JIMTOWN ROAD

JIMTOWN ROAD

A NOVEL IN STORIES

Winner of the 2016 Press 53 Award for Short Fiction

Dennis McFadden

Press 53
Winston-Salem

Press 53, LLC
PO Box 30314
Winston-Salem, NC 27130

First Edition

Cover art, "Forest Road," Copyright © 2015 by Dawn D. Surratt,
used by permission of the artist.
instagram.com/ddhanna

Printed on acid-free paper
ISBN 978-1-941209-43-1

"The meaning of life is that it stops."
—Franz Kafka

"In three words I can sum up everything
I've learned about life: it goes on."
— Robert Frost

ACKNOWLEDGMENTS

The author wishes to thank the editors of the publications where the following stories first appeared:

"All About Hearts," *Saranac Review,* Issue 7, 2011

"Dear Hearts, Gentle People," *Alfred Hitchcock's Mystery Magazine,* March 2014

"The Escapee's Lover," *The South Carolina Review,* Volume 45, Number 2, Spring 2013

"Jimtown Road," *New England Review,* vol. 23/number 3, Fall 2002

"Tickle Me George," *North Dakota Quarterly,* Volume 71, Number 1, Winter, 2004

"Tillie Dinger," *Ellery Queen Mystery Magazine,* March/April 2016

Contents

JIMTOWN ROAD

Freak Of Nature Brings Fear To Many Hearts Last Sunday
"...and fear, in more or less degree, descended
on the populace."
— *Jeffersonian Democrat*, September 28, 1950

Curly Smathers was not a little man, but the closer he got to home, the old farmstead carved into the forest north of Hartsgrove, Pennsylvania, the smaller he became. It was a week to the day after Black Sunday. Above his head, across the sky, a skein of geese pointed him homeward like an ancient arrow, Smathers following in an old Ford pickup, clattering over the rock-hard dirt of Jimtown Road.

Just ahead, where the road crested the hill, two girls turned to stare at the truck crawling toward them, pails a-droop from the clutch of their fists. The hilltop meadow, gold in the afternoon sun, commanded a sweeping view of the colorful crowns of the surrounding hills, where the woods blazed red and orange. At the crest, the two girls stood on the horizon, surrounded by blue sky, anchored by golden ground, halfway between heaven and earth, almost afloat. Smathers shivered at the grace of the vision. A squeal escaped the brakes as he pulled to a stop beside them, watching their stares go wide, their mouths fall open. Neither had ever seen a head so bald on a man so young, with eyes so bright and gay.

"Afternoon, ladies," said Smathers, flashing his jagged jack o' lantern smile. The older girl closed her mouth and nodded, the younger still showing the absence of her two front teeth. "Where you off to?"

"We're going berrying, mister," the taller girl said.

"Where bouts?"

"Grandpa says there's a big patch just over yonder by the edge of the woods."

"Oh," Smathers said. "Them's just blackberries—me, I'd sooner eat a nice fat bumbleberry any day."

"*Bumble*berry?" said the younger girl.

"*Umm* umm. Puts me in mind of sugar candy."

"Mister," the older girl said, "there ain't no such a thing as a bumbleberry."

"Why, there sure is," Smathers said. "Lady by the name of Carrie May—she was my stepmama—she showed me a patch of 'em one day when I was just about your age."

"What do they look like?"

"Bluer'n a blueberry—rasbier than a raspberry. Some of 'em's bigger'n your nose." The little girl's eyes widened again. The older's were full of doubt. "Who's your granddaddy?" Smathers asked.

"Perry McCracken," said the older girl.

"Heck, I know old Perry," Smathers said. "That's his place just down the road there a piece." The little girl nodded. "Why, I went to school with his boy Luke."

"That's my *pa!*" the little girl lisped.

"Sure, me and Luke goes way back," Smathers said. "What's your names?"

"I'm Mary Lou," the older one said, "and this here's my sister Katie."

"Nice to meet you, ladies."

"What happened to all your hair, mister?" Katie asked.

"Katie!" said Mary Lou.

Smathers laughed. "My papa calls me *Curly*."

"I'm sorry, mister," Mary Lou said, blushing for her sister. "Katie don't know her manners yet."

"Well, you ladies take care now. I believe I'm gonna go pick me some bumbleberries."

"*I* want to pick *me* some bumbleberries," Katie said.

"No!" said Mary Lou. Then, to Smathers, "We're gonna pick blackberries. Our Grandma's gonna bake us up a pie."

"Just as well," said Smathers. "It's a secret patch anyways. Carrie May made me cross my heart and hope to die I wouldn't ever show it to nobody else."

"He's just teasing you, Katie," Mary Lou said.

Smathers craned his neck to look up at the sky, an expanse so blue and clean he could not imagine it holding darkness. "Sure hope it stays light enough to pick 'em, though—heard tell it got mighty dark up hereabouts last Sunday."

"It was like nighttime in the middle of the day!" Mary Lou said.

Smathers nodded. "Musta been a little scary."

"Abner got scared!" Katie said. "He started in yipping and howling!"

"All the birds commenced their evening songs!" Mary Lou said.

"Pa thought the Russians dropped an automatic bomb!" Katie said.

"A*tomic* bomb," Mary Lou said. "Grandma got scared too—she figured it was Judgment Day coming."

"That's what that piece in the paper said," said Smathers. "I was setting in this here little diner in Paducah, Kentucky, last week when I seen this piece somebody was reading in the newspaper—said, *they thought the world was coming to an end.* Somebody'd drew a picture next to it, of where it got dark—looked like this long, black finger pointing me right back thisaway, right back toward home."

Smathers lit up his jagged jack o' lantern smile, and it grew. The sweet nostalgia of his homecoming filled him to the brim, and kept on filling, overflowing, spilling from his eyes. He was no longer small. How he grew, along with his smile. And still the filling went on. It was a moment so rare and euphoric that he'd experienced no other like it in his thirty years on earth; only once or twice had he come close. The whole sky filled him, all its vast and immaculate expanses, and he understood in some way beyond the reach of his knowledge the oneness of the universe and all that was in it, from the giddy heights of heaven to the two bewildered little girls standing before him.

At the bottom of the hollow, just past the plank bridge where the brook was the color of rust, Smathers Road forked off Jimtown Road, heading up the hill through the deep, cool shadows of the forest. On either side were banks knee-deep in lush fernery. At the top of the ridge, the road followed cleared pastures—Smathers wondered who farmed them now—to more woods, even thicker. These were the woods he knew, where he'd trekked for hours, gun in hand, bloody meat in his poke; these woods were virgin timber, dark and hilly, scattered with boulders like the marbles of God. They extended forever northward, becoming the great Allegheny Forest. Two miles up Smathers Road, the woods on the left thinned, then ended—more or less—where the first of the *No Trespassing* signs appeared, at the beginning of the old Smathers farm, eighty acres over four fields, now being reclaimed by the forest: young saplings and evergreens, thick undergrowth, a tide of browning ragweed speckled with Queen Anne's Lace. Up the easy slope, the road dead-ended at the farm.

At the sight of it, the memory of Carrie May stirred in his mind like a flower in the morning sun; the memory of the old man quickly followed, and his stomach rolled. He stopped the pickup where the road ended and the crabgrass commenced, near the burnt-out ruin of the barn. He was small again, incredibly small, the vast universe shrunk to this old farm house, boards weathered raw, tin roof curling to rust. He stepped from the truck, running a hand over his gleaming scalp, taking in the dereliction of the place: A few apple trees in the remnants of the orchard, and an unkempt garden near the house—scraggly corn stalks, tomato plants—were all that remained of the fertile acres, while the ragweed pasture beyond the charred relic of the barn hadn't been grazed upon in years. A scattering of scrawny chickens strutted and pecked. By the tilting outbuildings, a scramble of roses gone wild: Carrie May's roses. The surrounding woods inched closer and closer, a pack of wolves circling in for the kill.

He remembered going into the hen house the first time alone as a youngster to fetch the eggs; when the rooster had squawked up a ruckus and come straight for his face, he'd panicked and run, his heart slapping like the wings of the bird. Carrie May had marched him right back in again to face him down, insisting he be meaner than the bird. He'd left home, maybe ten years later, a couple of years after Carrie May was gone. It occurred to him that maybe he hadn't been leaving for the reason he told himself—to find Carrie May's aunt—maybe he'd been running away again. He felt his pulse reaching out to the tips of his fingers.

The old man stood on the porch, leaning into his stare. "I'd recognize that head o' hair anywheres!"

"Papa," Smathers answered, heading toward him. The old man came down the steps. A puppy scrambled down beside him, a brown, knee-high, yipping bundle of energy.

The old man sized him up. Big Vern was still bigger than his boy, who'd been Little Vern before he became Curly. The old man's cheeks were sunken, as were his eyes, frosty as his boy's were warm. His mustache might have dripped like dirty icicles from the ragged white thatch of his hair. Smathers was oddly comforted by the sight of his papa's shotgun, Old Aimee, still dangling from the crook of his hand.

"Your face looks familiar," the old man said, "but your feet has grown out of my knowledge." Then, to the puppy, still yipping, leaping like a trout around Smathers, "Bonehead, shut the hell up."

"Jesus!" Smathers said. "He's pissing on me!"

The old man nodded. "Happy to see you. We don't get much company."

"This here's a brand new suit."

The old man nodded again. Then he kicked the puppy hard, and the puppy yelped away across the yard. Smathers's ribs throbbed at the sight, old bruises rolling over. "Mighty fancy suit of clothes," said the old man, in his lusterless overalls.

Smathers shook his dampened leg. Neither man moved close to the other. "He your guard dog, is he?"

"Bonehead," the old man muttered. "So you're alive?"

"Alive and kicking," said Smathers. The old man spat in the dirt and turned back toward the porch. Smathers said, "Damn dog's happier to see me than you are."

The old man turned. His mustache rustled, hinting smile. "Hell, c'mon up. I'll be pleased to piss on your leg for you."

Smathers had to grin as he started toward the porch. Because he glanced down for the first step he never saw the old man's backhand coming, a wallop so hard it knocked him backwards, where he sprawled in the rubble of the yard.

The old man stood on the top step. "That's for running off. And never letting a body know whether you was dead or alive."

"Damn, papa," said Smathers, rubbing where the gnarled knuckle had torn his cheek. He felt like giggling, so giddy was he in relief and delight. "You made me rip the ass right out of my pants."

The old man nodded again, and Smathers thought he saw an actual smile this time. He *was* happy to see him. "Them fancy suits of clothes don't wear too good up here in the country," the old man said.

Smathers had worked up an appetite and his mouth was watering for fresh meat, not for the venison jerky and tinned beans begrudgingly offered by his papa. He set off with his old hunting rifle, a Marlin 30.06, down the easy slope of the wasted pasture, parallel to the road. He remembered sliding wild across the snow crust of this same field with Carrie May—he couldn't have been more than four— wedged between her knees in a cardboard box, her shrieks of delight as they tipped near the tree line and rolled laughing in a spray of snow. Carrie May was a splash of color on a gray slab of memory.

She'd been Carrie May Wonderling until, orphaned by a car crash on Sugar Hill, she'd married Vernon Smathers, recently widowed when his wife bled to death giving birth to Little Vern. Carrie May's age, halfway between that of Smathers and his father, made her an odd hybrid of sister and mother, daughter and wife. She was a small woman with large, capable hands, and a wide face full of eyes. When her eyes went big—in curiosity, concern, wonder, delight or any of a hundred other emotions that caused them to widen with every other blink—bright green irises floated free in pools of white.

When Smathers was ten, Carrie May's aunt brought her to Paducah to see Aimee Semple McPherson and her Foursquare Gospel Evangelical Revival. Carrie May came home converted. Her eyes were never bigger as she described the experience to her Little Vern—the glory and the joy—how she actually felt the Lord entering her body and taking her soul in His warm, loving arms. Then she set about, as Smathers later suspected her aunt had intended, the conversion of the old man and the boy.

The boy was an easy mark. Having lived all his life at the mercy of the moods and whims of an almighty father, the leap from papa-fearing to God-fearing was not all that great. He never knew when the wrath of the father might be visited upon him, when the cruel blows might rain down again—for a chore poorly done, for the look on his face, or for nothing but *being* in the middle of his sleep like a nightmare when the moonshine fumes hung heavy on the air. So he prayed with Carrie May because it pleased her, though he never knew for certain what became of the words once they left his lips, and nothing ever entered his body, that he could feel.

The conversion of Big Vern was less successful. From the first day Carrie May suggested he set aside his jug, the friction mounted. Little Vern sensed it for the most part, too young to see this cause or that effect, except for one: how much harder the old man now hit her. He'd never suspected him of pulling his punches before, when Carrie May, often as drunk as him, fought back, feisty and fearless, until afterwards, when she began turning the other cheek.

Then Carrie May was gone, simply swallowed up by the forest. Little Vern was thirteen, coming into manhood, and his papa thrashed him more viciously than ever, beating him for two, out of loneliness and rage, beating him for challenging his manhood by the mere claiming of his own, for pushing him headlong toward the grave. And almost overnight, not long after Carrie May was gone, Little Vern's hair fell out. Within a week, he was bald as Old Aimee's butt, and the wrath of the father was forever altered; it intensified, while becoming less physical. Having lost respect for him, he beat his boy less, cursed and derided him more, sneeringly calling him *Curly*, despising him for his perversion of the natural way of things, for his weakness, his softness and smoothness, for his seeming reversion to infancy—for challenging his manhood by the abandonment of his own.

Now Smathers was back, brought home by the long, black finger of God, to face down his demons. After her conversion, Carrie May told him she faced down her demons every day. She confessed to all her sins, past and present: drunkenness, waste, lust, wantonness—the latter two Little Vern had never suspected.

He remembered her chattering as she fried potatoes for breakfast in an iron skillet, his papa at the plain board table contemplating his cup and his jug, his overalls stinking of silage and muck. He remembered a prosperous farm, a hired hand, the legend of his great-grandpa Smathers clearing the land with an ax, a farm house trim and fresh. But his visions of the past and present farms were unconnected. They existed in separate times and worlds.

Smathers thanked God from whom all blessings flow as he spotted a doe and two fawns through the trees, grazing on the forest floor, tails working in nervous blinks. He crept into range, distracted by the breeze on his backside. Sighting down the barrel of his Marlin, the raw flesh of his wounded cheek was tender on the gunstock. Smathers squeezed the trigger, the doe dropping in a heap amid a shower of golden leaves before the report had finished echoing through the trees and off the boulders. He gutted her where she lay, then dragged her back through the woods. Emerging from the trees, the sun low in his face made it impossible to see beyond the moment, so he remembered Carrie May, unaware of the long shadow stretching out behind him, connecting him to the tree line, to the mountains beyond, to the very dawn of time.

They cooked venison steaks and roasting ears on an open fire Smathers built at twilight near the ruins of the barn. The old man butchered the doe, Smathers watching how he relished the wielding of the knife. After Smathers had rigged a spit to roast the meat and tucked the ears of corn into the red hot coals of the fire, he and his papa munched on soft tomatoes and stunted apples. It had been a hungry day's work. The old man never offered to share the jug from which he took his frequent pulls, so Smathers fetched himself water from the spring. Bonehead lay quiet and drooling, transfixed by the smell of the sizzling meat. After they'd eaten, Smathers foraged for dead wood to feed the fire as darkness spread over the farm, and they listened to the forest and fields come alive with the noises of the night.

"Where was you at last Sunday?" the old man asked.

"Illinois," Smathers said, "eating beans."

"Git dark up there? In the daytime, I mean?"

"Nope."

"Got blacker'n the inside of a grizzly here, middle of the day. I ain't lying. Got all dark and cold, but it wasn't no dark like night and it wasn't no cold like winter. Some kind of a sign, I figured—wasn't no good sign neither. I figured the Lord was fixing to call me on home. Why, I said hallelujah."

"Read where some folks believed it was World War III commencing," said Smathers.

The old man spat into the fire where it hissed. "Chickens all went to roost. Middle of the goddamn day. Old

Bonehead, he lays up there on the porch shivering in the corner like a coward. Quiet, too. Like a grave. I figured it was Doomsday come. I was listening for the trumpets."

"Hallelujah, papa."

"Chester Craven down at the store told me what it was was smoke. Forest fires up there in Canada. Wasn't true. You couldn't smell no smoke. I can smell a fire a mile away, and there wasn't a goddamn whiff of smoke."

Clear on the air came the sound of baying hounds, from the far ridge, miles off, carried close and loud by the echo over the hollow. Below, fog had begun to float from the ragweed, low puddles of cloud forming down the pasture. Hearing the hounds, Bonehead looked up from the bone he was gnawing and began to howl.

"Newspaper said it was fires too, papa. Must of been too high up to smell it."

"That wasn't no smoke, you little piss ant, you wasn't even here. What it was was a sign. Wasn't no good sign neither."

Smathers said nothing. Bonehead howled.

"Put me in mind of a bruise," the old man said. "First it gets all yellow, sickly yellow, then it goes to purple before it gets black. Like the worst shiner you ever seen in your life."

"You oughta be a expert on shiners."

"Wasn't just the sky, mind you. It was all around you. Almost like it was coming up out of the ground. Like you was setting here in the middle of a goddamn bruise."

"Like maybe the Lord give the whole world a licking?"

The old man stood to piss. Smathers saw a shooting star over his shoulder give a dazzling counterpoint to the puny, sputtering stream in the firelight. "Then you turn up."

"Lord works in mysterious ways," Smathers said. "Carrie May was always saying that."

"Bonehead, shut the hell up," the old man said to the howling puppy. But Bonehead howled on, at the far sound of the baying hounds across the hollow. "Half expected her. Figured maybe that's what the sign was for."

"She'll maybe turn up yet."

The old man took a pull from his jug. "She'll turn up all right. Come Doomsday, she'll turn up."

"And the earth shall pour forth its dead. Ain't that in the Bible? Something like that?"

"You'd have to ask Carrie May."

"Maybe she just up and run off. Like I done."

"She never would of left less she was dead. She needed me to beat the devil out of her. You might not of thought so, boy, but we got along pretty good. Even cats and dogs get pretty sweet on one another once they been laying down together a while. We kept one another in line. She was a mean little jigger, she was."

"So how'd she get dead, papa?"

Bonehead never knew what hit him. The old man caught him in mid-howl with the butt of Old Aimee, and he ran yelping into the darkness toward the house. "Goddamn puppies, never know when to shut the hell up," the old man said. "For a long time I blamed you."

"Blamed *me*?" Smathers ran his hand over his smooth scalp.

The old man nodded, and drank from the jug again. "I figure she got herself mauled by a bear up in the woods. Musta been a sick bear, maybe hurt. Then for a while I was thinking, if you'd of been with her like you usually was, like you should of been, that bear never would of took the both of you. But then the more thought I give it, I figured you're such a little piss ant anyways, he probably would of. Took the both of you."

"So you forgive me then? I thank you kindly."

They tried to pin it on him, the old man told him indignantly. He told him about the sheriff and his court papers and his bulldozer digging up half the farm, and Carrie May's kin—the Wonderlings from over in Dagus Mines—trying to burn him out, and the retaliations by Old Aimee and himself.

Smathers heard the baying of the hounds across the hollow growing louder. God works in mysterious ways. The old man's suspicions were contagious. The blackness *might* have been a sign; after all, hadn't it pointed him homeward?

"What brung you back?"

Smathers shrugged. "Ain't had nobody to call papa in a long time."

The old man spat. "So you done a little time, did you?"

Smathers was impressed by his papa's perception. "Done a little."

"What for? Spitting on the goddamn sidewalk?"

"For sticking a city slicker."

"What'd you stick him with? A hat pin?" The old man tried to chuckle, a cracked sound, the joy all withered out of it.

The sound of the baying hounds across the hollow grew louder still. It was too loud to ignore, but Smathers said nothing about it, and neither did his papa.

The old man stood with Old Aimee and a wobble, then bent unsteadily to retrieve his jug. He started toward the house. "When you leave, leave quiet. Me and Bonehead needs our beauty rest."

"So that's my homecoming, is it, papa?"

The old man turned and swayed. "Ain't your home no more, boy."

The fire popped and hissed, sending red embers dying toward the stars that speckled the black of the sky. Smathers made no connection between the dying embers and the old man, nor between the embers and the stars. He could only wonder at how so many points of light could try and fail to illuminate the night.

The hounds yowled on, an incessant mantra. From the porch, Bonehead soon took up the chorus, realizing the old man was safely inside.

Smathers lay on his back, awed by the first skyful of stars he'd seen in twelve and a half years. He drifted here and there on the pain and glory of the howling and the baying. Vividly in his mind, as much rumination as dream, Carrie May became Aimee Semple McPherson in a towering pulpit, arms outstretched like the wings of an angel, dazzling white robes flowing down like honey from heaven. Beneath the robes she was naked as the day she came into the world—naked as the day she departed. Naked as the woman he'd watched skinny-dipping in the moonlight. Her eyes of round delights shot lightning from above as the congregation cowered in awe, and trumpets sounded. She warned of damnation, fire, brimstone. Black smoke rose up all around her. She promised salvation, streets of heaven lined with gold. With the laying on of her hands, she could heal the sick, the infirm, the insane.

Could she also raise the dead?

Smathers had killed his mother claiming his own life. That knowledge had always fortified him, leaving him impervious to pain. From the porch, Bonehead's howl was full of terror, terror at the message of the hounds, terror at the smell of the smoke, terror at his utter inability to associate the wrath of the gods with his own howling, yipping, unalterable behavior. Smathers stood by the dwindling fire, stretching. Growing. Dew was beginning to dampen his new suit of clothes, and a half moon had topped the horizon. A few yards away the pickup hulked like a dark creature. Smathers went and lifted the tarp in the bed, like peeling back the night. A righteous chill of goose bumps swept up his back toward the pure, clean skin of his skull, where the moonlight glinted like a halo.

He walked toward the house, ten feet tall. Picking up a rock from the rubble in the yard, he crushed the puppy's skull. There was already blood from the doe on his pants, so a little more wouldn't much matter.

He wondered if the old man would hear him. He figured not; he figured him to be too deaf to hear thunder by now if he hadn't heard the ruckus of the hounds searching for the McCracken girls across the hollow. The Trumpets of Doomsday would sound, and the old man would miss them as well.

Sure enough, he never stirred as Smathers came into his room, tiptoed over Old Aimee, and sat on the edge of the bare bed where the old man lay shrouded in burlap. Moonlight cast a pale glow. In the shadows at the foot of the bed, Smathers detected the old butter churn, wondering for an instant why it was there before the image came to his mind of Carrie May, sitting churning on the porch, glistening with sweat, smiling, eyes wide and dancing. When his papa opened his eyes, Smathers held the glistening knife in front of his face.

He wondered if the old man could hear. "This here's the bone-handled knife I stuck that city slicker with, papa. Same one." Smathers lit up his jagged jack o' lantern smile, bigger than the night. He wiped the blade of the knife on the burlap. "Dragging that doe up through the woods there kindly put me in mind of Carrie May. Yes sir, papa. They say you always remember your first."

DEAR HEARTS, GENTLE PEOPLE

S heriff Foulkrod answered the call personally, two little girls missing in the woods off Jimtown Road ten miles north of Hartsgrove. They'd gone to pick blackberries. He pulled over amid a half dozen pickups, a battered old Chevy and a shiny Hudson coupe where the dirt road crested a hill. He left his red light flashing on the top of the cruiser. Dusk was settling over the wooded hills, muting the brilliant colors of early October.

Men were searching the woods, some women too. The girls' mother, Ethel McCracken, was waiting for him, and some of the older women were there, along with a young man, not dressed for the woods. Foulkrod didn't know him. Calls of *Mary Lou* and *Katie* echoed down through the hollow. The women rushed over. "Thank God you're here," said Ethel, a thin lady still wearing her apron, hair frazzled, eyes frozen as flint. It came to the sheriff then that there was no hope for the girls, by the look on her face: The mother always knows. "You got to find them, Sheriff," she said, despite what she didn't know she knew. "You got to do something."

Foulkrod did something: He got out of the car, rising to the full of his seventy-five inches, adjusting his glossy Sam Browne belt, patting his revolver, smoothing back his glossy hair, still mostly black, precisely positioning his eight point hat. He'd been sheriff of Paine County, Pennsylvania, for sixteen years, since 1934. "Don't worry, Ethel," he said, his coal-colored eyes gleaming kindly, "they'll be alright—just wandered too far in and got themselves lost," and a perceptible sense of relief settled over Ethel and the ladies. The young man was whistling a tune, which came to the sheriff: "Dear Hearts and Gentle People." Dinah Shore. It came to him because he detested the song, the way it always got stuck in his brain. Foulkrod questioned Ethel, made notes: Mary Lou and Katie, eight and six, dressed in blue sundresses, both dark-haired, both carrying shiny new pails, last seen around three. Katie missing her two front teeth. With his flashlight Foulkrod strode down and tromped for a while around the likeliest blackberry bushes, venturing into the woods a short distance conspicuously looking for clues—a pail, a shoe, signs of a struggle. He was content to leave the deep searching to those who knew the woods best, those who hunted there year round (with little regard to the official hunting season). After a while, he headed back up across the meadow. The women still clustered by the cars, wringing their hands, peering over the fields into the trees in the deepening gloom, as though they might be able to spot the two little girls from there. The young man whistled softly, arms crossed, staring at the woods as well.

The sheriff had done all he could do, though this he didn't share with the others. He retrieved his microphone from his dashboard, pulling it outside to talk so the others could hear. "Foulkrod calling, Foulkrod calling—Elizabeth? You there? Elizabeth?"

A woman's voice in a burst of static: "Here, Sheriff. What's your situation?"

"We're going to need some dogs—you want to see if you can raise the state police?"

"Oh, dear," said Elizabeth. "The poor things. I was hoping they'd be all right by now."

"They'll be all right," Foulkrod said. The women, the young man, were watching. "Soon as we get the dogs in to track 'em down. Just strayed too far into the woods is all."

Clipping the microphone back to the dash, the sheriff stood tall. The light on the cruiser still flashing, the red reflections were pulsing down across the deepening shadows of the fields. "Get some bloodhounds on the job," he announced. "Get 'em out of there in no time."

"I could see if it'd happened last week." It was the young man. He was thin and fair, wearing a sweater and khaki trousers. His hair was short and light, fuzz on his cheeks and upper lip, an attempted mustache and beard. They all knew what he meant, though no one said so.

The Sunday before was already famous: A massive cloud of smoke from Canadian forest fires, miles deep and wide and long, had drifted down over the whole countryside and beyond, blotting out the sun entirely. It had turned a bright Fall afternoon black as midnight, causing fear among the populace until the cause had become known, though, even now, the cause wasn't trusted. Even now, a sense of something unnatural, obliquely evil, still lingered. Black Sunday it was soon dubbed, and would remain. Equating that day to this one seemed wrong, a bad omen, a curse, a hex. "Do I know you?" the sheriff said to the young man.

"Raymond Shannon." He extended his hand, which the sheriff ignored. "I work up at the hospital. I stuck around in case they need some medical attention."

"You a doctor?"

"I'm a nurse."

"A nurse?"

"Yes. A nurse." Shannon ran his ignored hand through his hair, tucked it back under his arm. Down across the field, pulses of red flickered across the dark face of the woods. Men were straggling out, coming back up toward the flashing light. They hadn't been carrying lights when they'd gone into the woods in daylight.

"A nurse," the sheriff said. "The hell you say."

Perry McCracken, old man, half-deaf, came out of the woods. "Look it the circus lights up there—worthless slug of a sheriff finally hauled his fat ass out here." His normal tone of voice was akin to a shout. In the moment of silence, Ethel cleared her throat. "Where the hell's the dogs, anyways?" Perry said, presumably to his son Luke.

"Got a call in for the dogs," the sheriff yelled, so loud it raised an echo.

The two dark figures, Luke and Perry, hesitated halfway up. "He say they got a call in for the dogs?" Perry's whisper resounded. They made their way up to the cluster of cars.

It was nearly dark. "How you doing, Perry?" said the sheriff.

"Got my two little granddaughters out there in the woods lost," said Perry, short bony man, whisker stubble across a wrinkled face. "How the hell you think I'm doing?"

"I'm aware of that, Perry. What do you think I'm doing out here, anyways?"

"Not a damn thing, by the looks of it."

"Listen, I got a call in to the state police. We're getting the dogs out here. We're doing everything we can do."

"Well, do everything you can do in one hand," Perry said, "and shit in the other one—see which one fills up first." He spat on the ground.

"What the hell do you want me to do—call in the goddamn Marines?"

"Hell, yes! I want you to get out in them woods and find my little girls!"

"Hey." It was Shannon. "Fighting isn't going to help. We have to keep calm."

Everyone looked at him. We? An owl called out from the woods. Red light pulsed on the gathering night, flashing on the hard, frightened faces of men and women in denim and flannel. Stars began to poke through the nearly black blue of the sky. Foulkrod had been sheriff for many years and could understand Perry McCracken's fear dressed up as anger, but a young, male, whistling nurse in khaki pants he could not understand, and he was suspicious of what he could not understand. "Who'd you say you were again?" he said.

The young man said his name again. He looked away from the sheriff at the flashing red light, stared into it, and the way it flickered in his big eyes spooked the sheriff. Shannon said he'd stayed because maybe he could help if the girls were injured. The night had come down. The sheriff asked him where he was from, how long he'd lived here, asked him how he came to be in this neck of the woods in the first place, and the circle of men drew tighter around the skinny young man. His face grew calm and distant, red light pulsing in the peach fuzz.

"You were just driving by? On Jimtown Road? Cause the hills look pretty?"

"What are you saying, Sheriff?" said Luke.

"You ain't saying this little fellow knows something, are you?" Perry said.

Shannon said, "I was only trying to help." He started whistling again, "Dear Hearts and Gentle People," as he ambled away.

"Where you off to?" Foulkrod said.

"Back to my Aunt Jenny's—Jenny Pearsall. That's where I'm living." Everybody knew her, the old widow who lived just down Coolbrook Road a piece. Nobody liked her much. They watched the young man climb into his polished Hudson coupe, watched him back up, an awkward three-point turn on Jimtown Road, watched him drive off, red tail lights chased into the night by the pulsing red light of the sheriff.

Raymond showed up at my place, and I could see right away he was in a state. I asked him what was wrong. He shook his head. "What is the matter with people?"

"With people in general?" I said. "Or particular people?"

"Particular people." He threw a cushion across the room—high violence, for him. It bounced off the wall with a soft *plump*, doing damage only to Fauntleroy's nerves. The old dog was asleep on his rug in the corner and when the cushion landed beside him he jerked his head up, startled, afraid he might have to set his old bones in motion.

"Do you want to tell me what happened? Or just stand there and stew?"

The veins stood out on his forehead. He had that look on his face, big, hollow eyes staring right through you, expecting to see something that wasn't there. I'd seen that look once or twice in the few months I'd known him, when a particularly gruesome case had come into the Emergency Room where we worked. "Alice," he said, "you wouldn't believe it."

I got up and turned off the radio. Jack Benny didn't seem so funny all of a sudden. We sat on the couch and Raymond told me what had happened out on Jimtown Road, and he was right, I didn't believe it. I knew the sheriff of course—everyone knew the sheriff, or at least knew who he was, a big man who liked to be seen—and I knew who the McCrackens were, although I didn't know them well. I'd been in obstetrics when Ethel had given birth to Katie, so I remembered them. I might see her or Luke and the girls once in a while at the Golden Dawn getting their groceries, and Perry I'd seen up at the hospital a few times, mostly with cuts and bruises or a broken nose at the E.R. He tended to drink and fight quite a lot.

I said, "They weren't trying to say you had something to do with the girls getting lost, were they?"

"Not in so many words, maybe."

"Maybe you're overreacting. They're probably just frantic because of the girls, and said some things they didn't mean."

"Just because you're paranoid doesn't mean they're not out to get you."

"Was it just the two?" I said. "They have three daughters—Becky, Mary Lou and Katie."

"Just Mary Lou and Katie, is what I heard. The youngest two."

They were cute as buttons. I could picture them. Raymond couldn't, being so new in town. Schwab's dog down the road started to bark, probably a coon or a possum in the yard. Fauntleroy never budged, content to let the commotion take place without him. Fauntleroy was John's old beagle. John, my husband, was gone, had been for nearly a year, staying with an uncle in Dayton. Long story. John loved antiques, studied them, spent hours in antique shops, figuring to open his own some day. He was learning about buying and selling too, and that was what got him into trouble, when he sold one—a maple tea table, I remember—he thought, wrongly, someone had thrown out. They accused him of stealing it. How much trouble he was in he didn't stick around to find out. When anyone asked, I told them he was down south, looking for work. So there I was, alone in his hometown, with nothing but his old dog to keep me company—I tried to make the most of it, waging a one-woman war to keep from feeling sorry for myself. After all, a lot of people had it a lot worse than I did—just look at the McCrackens.

Schwab's dog chased the intruder out of his yard and, one last bark later, he was quiet. Raymond was sitting up, elbows on his knees, hands still clenched. I got up and turned on the radio. "Let's find some music," I said. "Let's calm you down." KDKA was playing hits. "Dear Hearts and Gentle People" was playing.

"Jeeze, Alice, turn it off—that damn song's been running through my head all day, I can't get rid of it."

"Now it'll be in mine all day. All night."

I turned off the radio and went to pick up the cushion he'd thrown. Even so, he kept humming the song. It's a small living room—John's old easy chair takes up most of it, in the corner by the Zenith like a hibernating bear. No one ever sits in it. There's an old wingback too, piled with junk I'm too lazy to put away—papers, mail, sweaters, and such—and the sofa, blue and green plaid with polished wood arms. The fabric reminded me of burlap, which is why I had cushions all over it. I picked up the cushion. Fauntleroy stirred, blinked, closed his eyes again. His eyes reminded me of Raymond's, only Raymond's lashes were longer.

Outside, a half moon over the hills gleamed on Raymond's Hudson. It was so quiet I could hear the engine ticking. He quit humming. "Maybe you should believe it," I said. "The part about how those dear people will never let you down."

He laughed. I hadn't meant to be funny, but he laughed so hard I had to smile. He slapped his knee and squeezed my hand. "Good one," he said, the laughing abruptly over.

"Do you want to spend the night?"

He looked up at me, not the look, the spooky one, but a new look altogether. He was looking into me. "With you, Alice Northey? A married woman? What will people think?"

"I didn't necessarily mean sleep together." Why did I say *necessarily*?

He leaned back, reached over, held my hand, but I could feel the tension. He didn't say anything. I glanced and saw the veins again, his jaw clenched where the peach fuzz gleamed in the shadow. Finally I said, "What do you want to do?"

"I want to turn back the clock somehow," he said, "and make those little girls safe. But I can't. Damn it, Alice, I *can't*."

The dogs didn't do any good. They never picked up the scent. When he knew the cause was lost, Foulkrod headed back into town, well after midnight, considerably slower than when he'd cruised out at dusk. Then, it had still seemed possible, even likely, the two little girls would be safe. They'd try again tomorrow, the dogs, the state police, the volunteers, but the sheriff didn't hold out much hope. A half moon was high in the sky and the pastures and meadows and forests were well lit on the way back to town, the stubble of mown corn glittering across the fields, and it was, he supposed, a fine thing to see, although it failed to lift the gloom that had taken hold of his heart.

He took his mike and pressed the button. "Foulkrod here. You still awake?"

Elizabeth's voice came through in the static: "I been waiting up—did you find them?"

"No. Nothing. Dogs never picked up a scent."

"How can that be? They can't just vanish like that."

"Can't they?" The sheriff rubbed the mike against his chin, stubble scratching. "I'll tell you about it tomorrow. It's late. I gotta get home and make sure my own little girl is all right." He could only imagine what Luke and Ethel must be going through right now, their little girls missing. His own daughter, Missy, was twelve—older than the McCracken girls, but not by much—and he felt a dull throb behind his heart at the thought of anything happening to her.

"Missy's fine, Bucky. Two little girls go missing in the woods doesn't mean anything's going to happen to her." The sheriff almost smiled. *Bucky*—Elizabeth's invention, he had no idea where it had come from; she was the only person alive who called him that, or could. "You have to keep your focus here—not to be critical, but sometimes you tend to internalize things too much. Something must have happened to them, if the dogs couldn't pick up a scent. They didn't just disappear into thin air."

"Yeah. You know, I wonder . . ."

"You wonder what? Was there something else?"

"Well, there was this young guy out there. Never seen him before." He told her about Raymond Shannon.

"A nurse?" she said. "Nobody ever laid eyes on him before, and he just happens to show up where two little girls have disappeared? What's wrong with this picture, Bucky?"

"Maybe."

They'd discuss it tomorrow, they decided, it was late. The sheriff respected the woman. She wouldn't be his dispatcher for long, he suspected; she'd taken the job (he suspected) only to learn the office before running for sheriff herself. Foulkrod could live with that; he had designs on a judgeship, having built up some solid Republican connections over the years. A woman being elected Paine County Sheriff might be a stretch, but if any woman could pull it off, it was Elizabeth Zimmerman. Meanwhile she and her husband, Ben, were busy acquiring coal and oil rights all over western Pennsylvania, busy acquiring a future and a fortune. Good people to know, good people to stay on the good side of.

He was thinking about Shannon, seeing the shiny Hudson fading into the black night, a slippery, elusive thing, when he pulled into his driveway at the end of Jefferson Street. Ruthie, his wife, was waiting up too, the lights still on in the living room. She came to the door to greet him, dressed in a crisp, pleated yellow dress with a broad, white collar, as if she'd just come in—or was just going out. She was still an attractive woman, blond, full-figured, fragile cheek and chin bones which she tended to hold high, as if she were trying to catch the scent of something distant. "What are you doing up, Butterlips?" the sheriff said, giving her a peck on the forehead. Over her shoulder, he saw her highball on the table by the sofa.

"I thought you might like some company when you got home." Her slur was soft and gentle. "Did you eat yet?"

She didn't ask where he'd been. "Maybe some warm milk," he said.

Ruthie warmed the milk while he changed, hanging his Sam Browne belt and the rest of his uniform neatly in what used to be the guest room, now his own private, locked space. Taking his Smith and Wesson from the holster, he inspected it for cleanliness. He placed his eight point hat on the dresser, shining the bill with his sleeve. Back out to the parlor in blue pajamas, he sat beside his wife, still fully dressed, and sipped his milk. "You going to change?" he said. "Or you going out dancing?"

"I don't feel like going to bed yet," she said, reaching for her highball. Lipstick smeared the rim, though the ice was hardly melted.

"Did you hear about the McCracken girls?"

"No. Should I have?"

"Two little girls up toward Coolbrook got lost in the woods. That's where I been."

"Oh dear," was all Ruthie said. She didn't ask if they'd been found.

"They're still missing," he said. "Out there in the woods all alone. At best. Is Missy all right?" Ruthie didn't answer. Her lack of empathy, her lack of concern about the McCracken girls disgusted him, but he could understand it: The drinking had numbed her heart as well as her mind. The drinking he could understand too, now that she was forty-five and fading fast, now that she'd grown immune to the pampering, was no longer the center of attention, enduring the long hours her husband was gone. Perhaps she'd never been cut out to be a sheriff's wife in the first place; at the banquets, balls and award dinners, in the spotlight, she'd shined, but when he was called away, so often the case, she was ill-equipped to cope, alone with an unhappy, defiant daughter. He pulled her close and stroked her hair near his chin, sipping his milk, listening to the ticking of the clock until his arm began to go numb. Ruthie never stirred, neither compliant, nor resistant, ice cubes melting slowly in the glass in her hand at which she steadily sipped. "Missy's asleep," she murmured into his shoulder.

"That's where I'm headed," he said, and she pulled away. "You too."

"The latch came loose on the screen door again," she said, her slur less gentle now.

"I'll fix it tomorrow. Come on—I'm putting you to bed."

"I'm plastered." She attempted to chuckle. "Like the walls."

She drained her drink, and he took her by the elbow, guiding her into their bedroom. He helped her into her

nightgown—she'd reached a stage of wooden clumsiness—
tucked her in and lay down beside her. The hours he spent
tucking in his girls. Turned off the light on the nightstand.
Ruthie was still, her breathing shallow. The door was slightly
open, a sliver of dim light from the hallway reaching across
the shadows toward his feet. "I better go in and check on
Missy," he whispered, his wife never stirring. He needed to
know his little girl was safe. Now more than ever, now, with
the nightmare of two girls all alone in a vast, black forest
roiling in his mind, now more than ever he needed to do
more than merely tuck her in. He needed to comfort her,
make her feel warm, loved and secure. He tiptoed toward
the door.

Behind him, Ruthie's prayer, slurred and mumbled,
from the bed: "Now I lay me down to sleep . . . you bastard,
you . . . dirty . . ."

I woke up to the smell of coffee, and for a minute I thought
it was John; he was always up before me, putting on the
coffee. Then I remembered, realized it was Raymond. He'd
spent the night after all, although not in my bedroom—
he'd slept on that awful, burlap-like sofa, somehow. It was
strange, another man in my kitchen. Odd, the places you
end up just putting one foot in front of the other. They
were opposites: Raymond was talkative, where John was
quiet, small where John was big, and, I suspected, cuddly
where John was, like most men I had ever known, pretty
much untouchable—I could only suspect because we'd
never cuddled. Raymond seemed above temptation. I got
out of bed and looked in the mirror. There were sounds
from the kitchen, a knife clicking on the counter top. I was
an attractive woman, not striking perhaps, but pretty
enough, or so I'd been told. My nose didn't amount to
much, but the size of my eyes, or so I'd been told, made up

for it. Looking at myself in the mirror, it suddenly came to me what I was doing—acting like a moonstruck bobbysoxer, trying to appraise my own desirability, when two little girls were horribly missing in the woods. I hadn't even thought about them since I'd woke up. I felt like such a muttonhead.

In the kitchen, Raymond was slicing potatoes. The skillet was already on the stove, a carton of eggs on the counter. "I hope you like a big breakfast," he said smiling over his shoulder, and when I went over to pour my coffee, I sighed and leaned against him and put my head on his shoulder, and he sort of froze. I said, "Those poor little things," and felt him relax, and we stood together like that for a moment or two. Outside, bright sunshine gleamed on the dew down the meadow, and a forest full of golds and yellows and reds stretched all the way to the horizon. How could a forest so beautiful hold something so horrible?

He had the radio on. "Did you hear anything?" I said.

"South Korean troops moving into North Korea. The Phillies won the pennant. Your poor Pirates finished in the cellar again—just the *real* news. Nothing about Jimtown Road."

"Oh dear." I started humming, "Dear Hearts and Gentle People."

"No!" cried Raymond. "No, no, God, no! I just got it out of my head—now it's back!"

"I'm sorry," I said. "Oh, dear."

"It'll be there forever now—till the day I die." He looked up, eyes twinkling. "Here's an idea—sing something else, before 'Dear Hearts' sets in—'Mule Train'! Let's sing 'Mule Train,' quick!"

"'Mule Train'? I hate that song."

"Come on! Sing with me, Alice—you started it—here we go: *Mule train, hippity-hopping over hill and dale—*

come on! You're not singing—*Doesn't seem they'll e-ver stop, hippity-hop, hippity-hop, hippity-hopping along! You're still not singing!*"

He was snapping his fingers for the whip snaps. "Good Lord," I said.

"Worth a try," he said.

Fauntleroy hobbled out of the kitchen, back to his rug in the living room, afraid of this suddenly crazy man. Raymond quit singing, but kept humming it, "Mule Train," dropping the potatoes into the skillet with a sizzle. I asked him how many eggs he wanted and got out a bowl and broke the eggs into it and beat them with a fork. We fixed breakfast like that, like an old married couple, without much chatter at all, the morning sunshine coming in through the window, and we sat and ate. He asked me what I was going to do that day. Laundry, I said. We were in no particular hurry, as we were on three to eleven. We didn't talk about the missing girls, not a word—what more could we possibly say?—but it was with us, there in the little kitchen, even more than John was. Much more, actually. I'd seen Raymond, the look on his face when he had to give a shot to a child, and it had always seemed to me that it was more painful to him than it was to the little girl or boy.

After breakfast we did the dishes. I'd have just left them in the sink, but he insisted. Washed, dried, and put away as well. Such a beautiful morning, we decided to take a ride.

We didn't talk about the McCracken girls even when we got into my Studebaker and headed out toward Coolbrook, past his Aunt Jenny's, instead of into Hartsgrove, even turning onto Jimtown Road. About a mile down, on the crest of a hill, there were cars and pickups pulled over on both sides, a lot of them, twenty or more. There were a couple of state police cars and the sheriff's cruiser. But no one was around. Nothing but cars. It was eerie. We stopped and got out and stood at the top of the hill looking down across the meadow to the woods. In the distance you could hear the baying of dogs. We stood there for a while, quiet, looking, listening. A deer bounded out of the woods and across the field along the far tree line. You'd have thought someone else would be there, but we didn't see another soul. Raymond drummed his fingers on the fender. "I'd be afraid I'd just get myself lost," I said.

"Me too," he said. "They'd just end up having to search for us, too." He crossed his arms. "And they'd never find us either."

When Elizabeth opined that a killer always returns to the scene of the crime, the sheriff said wasn't that just an old cliché?

Elizabeth said certainly, but clichés are clichés for a reason: "When something keeps happening, it keeps getting talked about, over and over and over again—that's how it becomes a cliché. So when they say a killer always returns to the scene of the crime, it's because it happens so often. Because it's so damn true."

They were having coffee at a corner booth in the Dixie Diner on Main. Foulkrod sat facing the interior, all red vinyl and chrome, Elizabeth across the booth. She was a pretty woman, thirty-five, wavy, midnight-black hair, skin like one of Missy's china dolls, teeth as white as her coffee cup. The sheriff noticed that everyone else in the diner couldn't keep their eyes off them, between him in his uniform, eight point hat on the hook by the booth, her in her navy-blue business suit, nylons gleaming on her legs. He was used to the glances.

"Now that you mention it," said Foulkrod, "first killer I ever arrested, Oscar Huffman, he was spotted back at the tower in the railroad yard where he'd done the dirty deed."

"I remember that. I was off at college."

"And here's this Shannon character, standing right up there bold as brass with all the women, while the men are searching the woods. Maybe he wasn't doing any searching himself because he knew there was nothing to find—maybe you're right."

"I'm not sure I even know him," she said. "Raymond Shannon."

"New around here, a little guy, pretty light in the loafers, if you know what I mean. Been staying with his Aunt Jenny—Jenny Pearsall, the old biddy—out toward Coolbrook. Says he's a nurse up at the hospital—I'll have to check it out. Says he was a medic in the army."

"So what are you going to do?"

"Not sure what I can do. Nothing, till they call off the search. I'd look pretty damn silly if I haul him in and those girls come walking out of the woods."

"You should put some pressure on him, sweat him a little, see what happens," she said. "What about his car?"

"Any clues'd be history. Looks like he spent the whole afternoon cleaning it up."

"Well, you can't just not do anything. Something like this happens, folks have to see you moving in some direction. And Shannon's the best direction you have to move in."

"You're getting pretty good at this stuff, aren't you?"

"I've been learning from the best, Sheriff." She smiled, but it was not the usual state of her face, which was soon solemn again. Tapping her cigarette on the edge of the ashtray, she shook her head. "Those poor little things. If it turns out he did do something to them, he ought to be, I don't know—castrated."

The sheriff nodded. "I was thinking fried, but I might like your idea better."

She nodded and they talked for a while about the suspicious young man and where he'd come from, who he might be, what he might have done, and they talked about ways to find out. When that topic had run its course they stood to leave, the sheriff dropping a dollar bill on the table, and Elizabeth asked if his little girl, Missy, was all right, he'd been so worried. He had to admit that sometimes he doted too much, and Elizabeth called him a big old mother hen. But she could empathize, her own little girl, Gloria, being just nine, and on the way out the door, out to Hartsgrove's busy, Monday morning Main Street, she straightened her hem, and began to sing a little song almost under her breath: "Dear Hearts and Gentle People."

He commented on the coincidence, said she sounded like Dinah Shore.

"Coincidence?" she said. "You've been humming it all morning, Bucky."

"I have?"

"You bet," she said, "and it's always been one of my favorites. Every time one of those gentle hearts leases away his gas rights to us in perpetuity for a pittance, Ben and I sing it all the way home. They certainly never seem to let you down, that's for sure."

"That's for *Shore*," the sheriff said.

Perry McCracken would never know what happened to his granddaughters. But then again, would any of us? A call came in one night that an ambulance was on the way, and we went outside to wait; it was bad, they said. The Emergency Room entrance was around back, a big curving drive carved into the top of the hill where the hospital was. We stood on concrete, a chill creeping into our bones. It was almost November. Raymond was wearing only his white nurse's shirt—I'd grabbed a sweater—and he hopped up and down in the chilly night air. There was a red pall over everything from the red light over the doors, and frost on the iron railing that curved away into the dark like a frozen snake. Raymond walked away toward the parked cars that were only glints and gleams in the dark, and lit a cigarette, still hopping, a little lonely dance. Ambulances usually carried something pretty gruesome to us, and normally we had a sense of dread, but I think he was almost looking forward to it now, the distraction, taking his mind off everything else. He'd told me that for three weeks the sheriff or one of his deputies seemed to be everywhere he looked. A couple of times one of their cars was parked overnight just across the road from his Aunt Jenny's. They talked to everyone he knew, to everyone in the hospital, and people were starting to look at him, people who hadn't before, in ways that they hadn't before. Mrs. Morley poked her head out and told us it was Perry McCracken they were bringing in, he'd wrecked his car out by the Halfway Turn on Coolbrook Road. I watched the news sink into Raymond. He stayed on the outer edge of the light where I couldn't see his face. He took a puff of his cigarette, the tip flashing big and red like the light above the door.

We heard the siren, faint at first. It grew, taking hold of us, and finally from the far end of the lot another light came around the corner, flashing from atop the ambulance, merging into the other red glow till it was a living, pulsing thing. Raymond came racing beside it, his arms spread out like wings, leaping, trying to lift off, and when the back of the ambulance burst open, we all got there together, Raymond, me, the attendant, Dr. Schaffer, the gurney hardly touching the ground, inside, scissors flashing, needles piercing, fluids flowing, blood running onto the floor, sponges, sutures, bandages, gauze, all in a whirl and a haze, and all too late, much too late, for Perry McCracken.

"That's what happens when you get too intimate with your steering post." Raymond tried to chuckle. "Another life lesson: Avoid intimacy." You have to laugh sometimes to keep from crying, he'd once told me. I couldn't do it. Poor Perry.

Day after day I'd tried not to think about them. Perry must have too. I'd tried not to imagine them all alone in the woods, the growling of the forest in the night, hour after hour, day after day, no father, no mother, no one at all to pick them up and carry them back home. Did they walk? Did they wander? In circles? Deeper and deeper into the woods? Did they pass close to a cabin, a road at some point, only to wander further away? Did they sit and wait? Rattlesnakes. There were millions in the woods. Bears. Mary Lou must have comforted Katie. Must have tried to hide her own awful fears. Day after day. Did one of them die first? Was one left alone? What an awful thing when it happened, when you realized that the best thing to hope for now was not that they'd be rescued, but that they hadn't died horribly.

Raymond seemed to arrive at that place before me. I tried to hide the tears one day when he walked into the kitchen and caught me crying. The sheriff had stopped at my house too, and a deputy had visited me at the hospital another time. They wanted to know how well I knew Raymond, how long I had known him. They wanted to know anything, everything, I knew or could guess about him. When Raymond found me crying, he knew why; I didn't have to tell him. We'd never talked about the girls after the first couple of days, until then, and even then we didn't really. He took me by the shoulders and fixed me with that stare, and I don't know what he expected to see. "They're home now, Alice," he said. "At peace. Beyond care. Just love them."

How could he know? What did I know? How well did I know him at all?

They were watching their little girl swim. In the time that followed the vanishing of the McCracken girls, many parents watched many children do many things they hadn't watched before. A balcony, not much wider than a walkway, ran along the wall beneath the high dirty windows above the Y.M.C.A. swimming pool, and that was where they stood in the chlorine-saturated air, along with a half dozen other parents, listening to hollow echoes, watching a dozen kids in the pool down below. The other kids looked up smiling and waving from time to time. *Watch this, Mom, look at this, Dad.* Not so, Missy. Missy didn't look up.

Ruthie smiled and waved at her daughter who wasn't watching. She said, "Just because he might have done it doesn't mean he did." They'd been talking about Shannon. As far as the sheriff was concerned, Shannon was responsible for a third death now, old Perry McCracken.

"Somebody's always responsible," said the sheriff. "You got anybody else in mind? Who? You suppose some alien swooped down out of the sky in a flying saucer? Who?"

"The week before," Ruthie said, "it turned into midnight at noon."

"What does that even mean?" the sheriff said. The iron rail around the balcony was sweating where he put his hand on top of his wife's. "You can put that midnight-noon notion right out of your mind. That never happened before and it'll never happen again, and it might as well never have happened at all."

"You have to believe in magic," she said.

He couldn't be bothered. She didn't understand. All he wanted to do was watch his girl. He couldn't believe how beautiful she was, as seen from on high, the perfect legs and arms and body, the strawberry hair flowing out in ripples, the body that he'd created. A rush of blood ran through him. "In the real world, there is no magic. If it looks like a duck, quacks like a duck and walks like a duck, then it's a goddamn duck. No magic about it. The man's a monster."

Missy looked up, waving them off with her hand. "Go away!"

The sheriff and his wife waved and smiled. "Don't ducks waddle?" Ruthie said.

"Waddle, walk, whatever. Don't you worry your pretty little head."

"Why don't you shoot him?" Ruthie said.

The sheriff nodded thoughtfully. "He deserves it, but certain niceties have to be observed first. Bring him in, sweat him, try him, then fry him." He squeezed Ruthie's hand, his own touching the slimy railing. He pulled it away, took out his handkerchief and wiped his hand. Missy swam to the shallow end of the pool, stood up and yelled again toward the sheriff and his wife, "Go *away!*" They smiled and waved back.

"Would you like me to?" Ruthie said.

"Like you to what?" They watched Missy swimming.

"Shoot him. Kill him. Take your six-gun and stop him from hurting little girls."

Foulkrod smiled. "Would you do that for me, Butterlips?"

"Would I ever," Butterlips said.

They arrested Shannon two days later at the hospital in the middle of his shift, took him away in cuffs, blindfolded him, transported him north to the Sugargrove state police substation, brought him down to the infamous interrogation room in the basement, turned on the bright lights and grilled him for hours. They brought in their best detectives, grilled him in shifts. After nearly two full days, however, Shannon hadn't given an inch. In fact, the sheriff told Elizabeth later, he took to whistling "Dear Hearts and Gentle People" just to piss him off.

"He's one tough little son of a bitch, I'll give you that," he told Elizabeth.

"Kind of proves the point then, doesn't it?" Elizabeth said.

After they took him away I lay in bed one morning half awake and half asleep and dreamed about how strong he was: I'd seen him lift a two hundred pound man all by himself, more than once, and blood didn't bother him at all, he waded right through it. That's what made him so good in the E.R. In my dream, or daydream, he was fantastic, tipping back a boulder to see if the little girls were lost underneath it. When he didn't find them, he looked over at me. He kept looking through me, straight through to the back of my head and beyond, his eyes like sunbeams, then he crossed his arms, a deer bounded away, and the last thing he said to me before Fauntleroy scratched at the door and brought me awake was *they'll never find us either.*

A premonition, maybe? I got up and let the dog out, came back in, put on the coffee and got dressed. I was wondering about Raymond and the dreams or half-dreams or whatever they were, when I heard a car pulling into the driveway. Fauntleroy barked his wheezy old bark. It was Raymond in his Hudson.

I should have known he might show up, but I wasn't ready. I put my robe on over my dress and went to the door. He stopped on the stoop when I didn't ask him in. He didn't ask if he could come in either, just said he'd come to say goodbye. There were no smiles. The hospital had let him go, we all knew that. "What did they do to you?" I said.

"You don't want to know." He was right. He looked gaunt and frayed, even skinnier, the veins permanently imprinted on his forehead, or so it seemed. "I just want you to promise you'll never shop at Sears Roebuck again." I looked at him and frowned.

"Their catalog attacked me," he said, "whacked me on the head at least a hundred times." It was the only hint he gave of what they'd done to him.

"I'd ask you in," I said, "but I'm not dressed yet."

He nodded, said, "So I see," and looked me up and down. There was an awkward little lull. Then he asked if I remembered the trout. We'd walked in summer up on Potters Creek, up into the woods, and we were both watching the same spot on the water up above the dam where it was widest when a trout jumped out, and we both happened to see it at the same time. Funny too, because I'd told him about all the times John had dragged me fishing up there with him, and we'd never caught a thing. Now there they were, taunting us. I said yes, I remembered, and I tried to smile. "For some reason I thought of that trout," he said. "I'm still dizzy, I guess."

I asked him what he was going to do. My heart was fluttering, my skin crawling and I hated him and I hated myself. He was staring that stare, looking right through me. He said he was going to say goodbye, get in his car and drive to Mars, and then he said, "Alice, you know I can see you crying. I can see the tears in your eyes from way over here."

"I am not crying."

"And that's not all I can see," he said. "I can see your dress poking out from the bottom of your robe." He pointed, started to back away, wagging his finger, turning it into a wave.

I closed the door. I waited till his car door slammed so he wouldn't hear me, then I locked it. His car didn't start right away. I heard him start to sing: "Dear Hearts and Gentle People." He sang in a loud voice, a stage voice, almost a shout, mocking, how he loved the gentle people from his home town, how they would never, never in a million years, let him down.

He drove away. Even though he was gone, even though he couldn't see in, even though I was safe, I still drew the curtains.

Twilight in early December, Sheriff Foulkrod stood beside his cruiser, the flashing red light playing across the overgrown fields of the abandoned farm, pulsing on the burnt-out ruin of the barn, the weathered boards of the derelict house. A place too forsaken for ghosts. A pair of state police cars were parked near his, the coroner's van, men in uniform walking in and out of the house, all through the rubble of the yard. A skeleton of a dog on the porch. Foulkrod raised Elizabeth on the radio.

"Yes, Sheriff, here. What is your situation?"

"The Smathers," the sheriff said, "you remember them." More statement than question, as she certainly did. Everyone did. They were as reclusive and mean a brood as any of the hillbilly tribes over past Dagus Mines, and they had been for a hundred years, though their numbers were dwindling now toward zero. "Found ol' Vern dead in his bed—probably been that way a good two, three months. Not much left of him after the critters got done, but still enough to see the nick on his spine where his throat got cut."

"My goodness," Elizabeth said.

"Your goodness, all right," he said. "Just across the hollow from Jimtown Road. Killed about the same time the girls went missing. Chester Craven down at the store says Vern's boy Curly was seen in the area right around the same time too. That's one mean, crazy son of a bitch. You know what? That's too big a coincidence. I'm thinking now it might not have been our boy Shannon after all. Matter of fact, I'm thinking it probably wasn't."

"Listen, Bucky, that still doesn't mean he didn't do it. He *still* could have done it."

"All the same," said the sheriff. "I don't know." He looked around him, at all that lay dead and in ruin. "Probably just as well Butterlips didn't go out and shoot him for us, though."

FORGET-ME-NOTS

For the first few months after her operation, John tried to spend more time with her, long afternoons in her house at Cranberry, cuddling to the best of their ability, watching television, staring at the stained glass bluebird in the kitchen window, in silence much of the time. Laughter seldom came to the rescue as it had so often in the past. Toward the end, Lena was too weak to reach up to open her mud-colored cupboards, so her Wheaties and Uncle Ben's and cans of Campbell's sat scattered on the counter tops, untouched for days. She'd been a lanky woman with clear, gray eyes, eyebrows darker than her sandy blonde hair, but by then the eyes were clouded, the lankiness that of a scarecrow. The *Closed* sign was back on her shop door, the same as on his own, miles away in Hartsgrove, their businesses fading and all but forgotten. The few times they made love, she never took off her shirt.

The last time he saw her, the scarf over the stubble that once was her hair, white pasty face, what could he say? By then the chemo had defeated her. They couldn't cuddle, she hurt too much and he was so big, lying in her bed, dusty curtains, gray light. He was a large man with a close-cropped beard he'd grown at her suggestion to offset his big, round moon of a face, the face, she said, of a mischievous little boy. Dark, thick, unruly curls of hair. He heard an owl outside. Middle of the day, odd time to hear an owl. Had she heard it too? *Did you hear that?* he said. *Who?* she said. *There's an owl—I heard an owl outside. Who?* she said. *An ow—oh, my God,* he said, but by then it was too late, he'd already missed it, her joke, her last joke, and the look on her face was the look of someone who couldn't quite reach the life saver that had been thrown her, and she was going under.

He didn't see her after that. After she'd gotten too sick, after they'd given up on the chemo altogether, after her sister had moved in to take care of her, and she'd gone back to the hospital, he never saw Lena again.

He just couldn't leave his wife. His wife, Alice.

He remembered the green of that day. An overcast day in late May and when he left her, looking for the owl on the way to his car, the fat green leaves of the maples and elms in the yard, the pines in the tree line across the green pasture, the shrubbery, the laurel and rhododendron, all so brilliant in the diffused, diminished light, overwhelmed him, shades and shades of green, light, dark, lemon, lime, apple, rich, thick, luxurious, infusing him, trying to suffocate him. What it felt like was an accusation.

He'd met Lena in Sharon, Pennsylvania, in 1950, just over ten years before that last afternoon. At the time, he'd been on the run, staying with his Uncle Richard in Dayton. Though his crime had not been particularly egregious, he'd nevertheless fled Hartsgrove, leaving behind Alice, his wife of only a year. Was his crime his only reason for fleeing? Or was there also an element of newlywed dread, of panic? Whatever the reason, his Uncle Richard disapproved, disapproval etched like a banner on his forehead every day. His uncle was a prudish man who lived alone, a mid-level banker who wore dirty tweed vests.

John had always loved antiques, the smell of them, the look and the feel, perhaps due to his sentimental nature, his penchant for nostalgia. Phil Bish, an old family friend, was in the business, owned his own shop, Forget-Me-Nots on Main Street in Hartsgrove, probably a formative factor as well. After the war and a brief, terrifying stint at college on the G.I. Bill, John was selling insurance, or trying, spending much of his spare time helping Bish (who was getting older, while John was big and young and strong, and didn't mind the heavy lifting intrinsic to the trade), studying the business, hoping someday to open his own shop. He'd come across an old maple tea table abandoned at the curb after a yard sale up on Pine Street. He saw value in the grain and patina and craftsmanship, features in which Bish had schooled him, and he took the table, proudly bringing it to Bish's, selling it on consignment. John's first foray into the business did not end well, however, when the table turned out not to have been as abandoned as he'd hoped, and he was charged with its theft.

From Dayton one day he drove to Sharon for an antiques show he'd seen advertised. There he first saw Lena, admiring a Nantucket sideboard, touching it sensuously, and for some reason (he was not always so bold), perhaps the way she was standing with her hand on her skinny hip, the way her hip was pointing at him, he'd wisecracked, *Say, that reminds me of a Limerick.* The best he expected was an icy glance, if not outright rebuke. Instead she'd laughed. Not a miniature snicker or giggle, but a full-hearted laugh of robust proportions. Love at first sight. They talked for a while, him with his new-found ability to charm tall buildings in a single bound, and they went to dinner. Even then it might have gone no further if he hadn't managed somehow to spill his plate of spaghetti onto the lap of his khaki pants. They went to her room at a nearby Howard Johnson's to clean up, but what were they supposed to do while his pants were drying? By then, they'd known each other for years.

He was a year on the lam before he'd finally grown up enough to go back home and face the music. The music turned out to be a five hundred dollar fine, six months' probation. By then, he and Lena were in love. By then too, he and Alice were over two years married.

The first time he saw Alice he was in serious pain. He'd damaged his back, as well as his youthful illusions of invincibility, wrestling a massive roll-top through the doorway of Forget-Me-Nots. Alice was a nurse at Hartsgrove Hospital, high on one of the town's seven hills, and he scarcely noticed her at all, just another white uniform. The next time he saw her, however, it was his heart that was in serious pain. His back had recovered, but a girl named Suzanne, whom he'd met and fallen for at the nearby state teachers' college had dumped him, and he was nursing his wounds, searching for solace in a platter of meatloaf and mashed potatoes at the Dixie Diner. He noticed Alice sitting alone in a corner booth, trying to be invisible, picking at a salad, looking through the window at twilight falling on Main Street. The plain and pretty face looked familiar, doe eyes and brave little nose, but it took him a while to place her. Then he remembered: the nurse. She looked lonely and troubled, feelings with which, for the first time in his life, he could easily identify.

Suzanne had blindsided him. He'd been stationed in Washington during the war, had experienced his share of big city life, of flings and encounters, considered himself worldly enough and wise, and when he came back to his little home town and enrolled in the college a town over, he was on top of his game. Suzanne was in his business class and they'd drifted together, magnetism of a sort, studying together, snacking at the campus hang-out (a favorite was root beer floats), going to the movies downtown. After *Abbot and Costello Meet Frankenstein,* she inadvertently followed him into the men's room, a faux pas he wouldn't let her live down. They seemed to fit together so well, so effortlessly, that he was astonished when she kissed his cheek (his big, round, naked cheek) one spring morning and told him goodbye. She was leaving school, moving back to Pittsburgh. She was homesick. She missed the lilacs in her backyard.

"What about *us?*" he asked.

"I care about us," she said. "But not enough to stay."

John carried his meatloaf, mashed potatoes and root beer float to Alice's booth. "Remember me?" he said.

Alice looked up from the window with hungry eyes. "How's your back?" she said.

He was a sophisticated vet fresh from college and the big city, back in his little home town, she was from the hills beyond Dagus Mines, a newly-minted nurse to whom Hartsgrove was as big as Washington had been to him. On their first date, at the Moonlight Drive-In, they missed most of *The Sands of Iwo Jima*—Alice allowing John to go much further than she'd intended, forgetting she was wearing falsies, nearly dying of mortification. But John made her laugh. *I think I found your earmuffs,* he said. He clapped them on his ears. *How the heck they got inside your shirt*

I'll never know. He was wonderful. He made the great mistake of letting her fall in love with him, and so, eventually, he proposed. After Suzanne, he knew he'd never truly fall in love again, and, while he was fond of Alice, mostly he wanted to protect her. He did not want her to have to suffer the heartbreak he'd endured. It was a brave and noble thing to do.

A year or two before John met her at the antiques show in Sharon, Lena had become a widow. Her husband, Wendell, proprietor of Classic Antiques in Cranberry, had been crushed to death by a classic antique floor safe when he and his cousin were wheeling it up a ramp and it tipped over on him. He'd been a little guy. The safe weighed almost a ton. No contest. Lena took over the business. John sometimes wondered about her husband's death. Assuming the cousin in question hadn't been a hired assassin, then it seemed to him natural selection must have played a role, and if so it worked: they'd never had children. Though she sometimes grew pensive at a mention of him, Lena never seemed to mourn the man to any great degree. Nor did it seem to trouble her that the murder weapon, an 1870's Herring and Farrell parlor safe, was still sitting in her store, still for sale. What was she to do? It was a two thousand dollar item. She was nothing if not pragmatic.

He told her from the start, within the first half hour, that he was married. No pretenses, no lies, everything up front and above-board—as above the board as an illicit affair can be. He told her all along he couldn't leave his wife; Alice had done nothing wrong. He couldn't wreck her life when she'd done everything that was expected of her, everything she'd promised to do. Suzanne, he kept to himself. He didn't tell Lena what had happened to him, and how he had tried—was still trying—to keep the same thing from happening to Alice. His feelings of nobility were increasingly tainted, however, by suspicions of cowardice.

They would still be able to see each other. Cranberry and Hartsgrove were only fifty miles apart, they were both passionate about antiques, there were shows and sales and flea markets and auctions and odd hours, and Alice worked, and Wendell was dead.

There could be only one graceful solution: if Alice met someone else. She was young, somewhat pretty, and perhaps someone else had been sucked into the vacuum created by his absence. That would be the best that could happen, Alice meeting someone else, because then he could leave and go with a clear conscience to Lena. No mess, no fuss, no heartbreak for anyone. The best possible possibility, a slim hope at most, but when he returned from his exile in Dayton, Alice was overjoyed to see him, she'd missed him terribly, and nothing about her hinted at anyone else. Then one night he stopped at Jum's for a beer.

A venerable dump on Main Street, Jum's was the scene of his first legal beer, and he thought he might reconnect with an old pal or two, maybe Timmy Martin, with whom he'd joined the army; he'd returned from Dayton not exactly on the sly, but under the radar. If nothing else, he could use a comfortable dose of local color, Doodle O'Hanlon maybe, or Doodle's pal, Weasel Fleager. But it was Wahoo, local color in her own right, who was there that night.

Wahoo, whose mostly unknown name was Rita Schreckengost, was part German, part Indian, all drunk, and delighted, loudly, to see him. She wanted to dance. The juke box, nearly as loud as Wahoo, was playing Hank Williams, "Cold, Cold Heart."

"Whoa, whoa, Wahoo—I'm a married man, remember?" She tugged on his hands. "Well that don't stop Alice now, does it?"

"It don't?" He wished he'd been more eloquent.

According to Wahoo: Alice had been stepping out with some fellow, a nurse up at the hospital with her. He'd spent the night at Alice's, more than once. Wahoo knew this because her best friend, Mary Lou McAninch, lived just down the Coolbrook Road from John's and Alice's place. "You're shitting me," said John, again with unfortunate lack of eloquence.

"No I ain't," said Wahoo, her eyes losing focus, "c'mon, let's dance!"

He declined, as politely as he could, his heart flying, his head swimming.

Wahoo's view of the world being classically unreliable, he needed verification. Could it really be real? Do dreams really come true? Of course the idea of being cuckolded was not very flattering to his self-esteem, but he was man enough to swallow that bitter pill for the cure it promised. Perhaps Alice had feigned her joy at seeing him again, biding her time, waiting for the right moment to let him down gently, to tell him about this fellow, this nurse. About her and this fellow. Perhaps *she* had been fearful of hurting *him*. John could only hope.

And verify. He turned to the first source at hand, at the end of the bar: Doodle O'Hanlon, clear-eyed old rummy, had occupied that barstool forever. What's more, every rumor that had ever run through Hartsgrove had passed through Jum's. But Doodle proved to be an unlikely source of intelligence. He didn't remember any male nurse—he swore in fact that men weren't allowed to be nurses. Jum himself, in his rotund and dirty white apron, proved to be no use either. He wouldn't pay much mind to small town rumors, he said. Small town folks had nothing better to do than wag their tongues and rattle their jaws. But did John detect a reluctance in Jum to look him in the eye?

John finished his beer and went out into the sticky summer evening where the clock high in the dome of the Court House across the street said eight-fifteen. Forget-Me-Nots was still open. Phil Bish was a friendly, outgoing fellow with a popular shop on Main, the geographical center of the rumor mill, but should he ask him? His mentor and friend, John had known him almost all his life—before his father died, before Phil's wife died, when John was a kid, the Bishes and Northeys had socialized, Saturday night dances at the Eagles, Friday night fish-fries at Vowinkle, pinochle and canasta. This was before John and Phil became estranged, before John opened his own shop on the other end of Main and they became rivals, before John began to wonder if Phil shouldn't have suspected something wrong with the whole stolen-tea-table caper, and warned him off, imparted some actual wisdom and guidance. When John turned to him that sultry summer evening, Phil dismissed the whole rumor as utter nonsense, telling John he was a God in Alice's eyes, one she couldn't live without—a dismissal suspiciously glib.

John turned to his mother, Edna. He'd known her when she'd known everything, and sometimes he thought she still did. She lived in the same little brick house his father had bought thirty years ago—his dad had been dead five years by then—on Oak Street, a quiet hometown street in a quiet neighborhood, tidy homes, neat lawns, sheltering oaks and maples. There was a pine grove behind the house where John and Chuck, his kid brother, and the neighborhood kids used to play on the soft carpet of pine needles. For the rest of his life, the smell of pine would remind him of home, and of Chuck crying. Crybaby Chuckie, always crying.

John and his mother were close, especially since his father had died and Chuck had moved away. His father had been a mailman, far from an ideal job in Hartsgrove which was built on seven hills. Steep hills. He'd walked up and down the hills, walked and walked, one foot in front of the other until one day he took one step too many and his heart said, *Enough!* and quit, and there was his dad, RIP in a flourish of junk mail and flyers. As for Chuck, he'd wanted to stay in Hartsgrove, but his bride's family lived near Pittsburgh, and so now he did too. If there was a meaningful trend in how the Northey men always seemed to yield to their women's wants, John succeeded in ignoring it.

Edna had her feet up, listening to the big old floor-model radio beside her, on top of which her ashtray overflowed. The Pirates were on. Ralph Kiner was up. Edna raised her hand, warning John to silence pending the outcome of the at-bat. Pall Mall smoke in the air thicker than at Jum's. Her blue bandana was still in her hair—she liked to tie it back, keep her hair out of her face while she was at work, at her beauty shop down on Main. "You lost, little boy?" she said after Kiner struck out.

"Just happened to be in the neighborhood," he said.

"Help yourself." His mother waved her brown bottle.

"If I must." After he'd retrieved a beer and sat in the rocker across from his mother—the rocker had been her chair, the overstuffed monstrosity by the radio in which she was now sitting had been his father's—he told her he'd just come from Jum's, that Wahoo had been there (his mother loved the local color too), and that she'd told him a rumor. He told her the rumor.

"The nurse's name was Raymond," his mother said. "Raymond Shannon."

"So it's true?"

"Did I say that?" His mother's was a smoker's voice, gravelly, gruff, always this close to sarcastic. Long lashes fluttered over clear eyes. "You sound like you want it to be true."

It was that obvious? "I just want to know where I stand."

"What did you think she was going to do while you were off playing cops and robbers in Dayton? After you left her high and dry?" While he was gone, Edna told him, Alice had turned to Edna—she had no one else, and so maybe she'd turned to Raymond, too. Edna had had her over for supper a few times, and once, maybe twice, Raymond had come with her. He seemed to be a nice young man, a little light in the loafers perhaps, but friendly, polite. He'd had his own run-in with the law, a total misunderstanding, and had left town rather abruptly.

"I heard he spent the night with her," John said.

"Oh you did, did you?"

"Did he?"

"Sorry." Eyelashes fluttering scorn. "I forgot to follow them around."

"Well, what am I supposed to think?"

"You're supposed to think if you walk out and leave your wife, she might get lonely. She might need somebody to talk to. But as for Alice, poor little thing, I'm not so sure she'd have the wherewithal to know how to cheat on a man."

Poor little thing came home after her three-to-eleven shift, weary and ready for sleep, her crisp white uniform soiled and limp, only to find John waiting, softly accusing. Though their voices were more mournful than loud, Fauntleroy, the old dog, slunk from the room to find peace in the next. Their place on Coolbrook Road was where the town ended and the country commenced, and a wolf howled in the night, hauntingly, somewhere in the woods behind the house. *I didn't deserve to be his friend* was what she finally decided about Raymond, and John didn't want to hear more, as she had told him everything he needed to know. He suspected his mother was right about Alice's wherewithal. Alice, though,

was sad, apparently considering her friendship with
Raymond to have been a betrayal of sorts of John, and even
though he was drunk, or nearly drunk, which she didn't care
for, she made it up to him, even though she was too tired,
she made love to him in her eager, awkward and anxious
way, and by the time the salty sweat had dried on their
sleeping skin, all hope was gone.

Years. Alice remained devoted. A son, Georgie, was born.
From where John stood, there never was—never could be—
another man, though once in a while he brought Raymond
up, just to remind her the ghost of suspicion still lingered.
Or to remind himself? He came to believe that only one
alternate graceful solution, one other way out, truly existed:
until one of them—him, Alice, or Lena—was dead, the
dilemma would endure. Not a happy hope.

On their tenth anniversary, in a room in the Howard
Johnson's in Harmony Mills, he told Lena about Mrs.
Chestnut, who'd come into his store, Northey's Antiques,
that day. It was the sort of story they loved.

Mrs. Chestnut was a short, squat, lady who walked with
a waddle. *Try to picture Elmer Fudd as an old lady,* was
how John described her, which made Lena laugh, which in
turn made champagne spray out of her nose. Good comedy
is all about timing, and John couldn't deny he knew Lena
would find the line funny, nor that he'd waited till the sip
was in her mouth to use it. He was crazy about her sense of
humor, as well as other parts of her body. They'd long since
arrived at the place in their relationship where they could
amuse themselves in a secret code that would have been
undecipherable to anybody else, if anybody else had ever
been there to try to decipher it—an expression or a gesture,
lifting an eyebrow, flipping a wrist, or one of the abbreviated

punch lines that had distilled over the past ten years: *does this make my ass look fat?* for example, seldom had anything to do with trying on clothes.

John had perked up when Mrs. Chestnut came in. She was not a browser but a buyer, a person who made actual purchases. Last month she'd purchased the Medici secretary-hutch with the traditional chicken-wire front for nine hundred dollars—he'd marked it at eleven, hoping to get eight. When she gave him a wave and headed for the bathroom in back, he turned up the radio, ever the gentleman, as there were no other customers in the place, no other noise, and the last thing he needed was an audible fart that might drive her, embarrassed, from the shop. At this, Lena laughed. Mrs. Chestnut came back out to browse, and, before long, sought out John to ask him about the Provencal walnut desk. As he was following her toward the desk, he noticed it: a trail of toilet paper dragging behind her, from underneath her dress.

"What the hell do you do?" John asked Lena, rhetorically.

He couldn't take his eyes off the thing, trailing along the floor in her wake. Her calves above her high heels, John noted, were white, fat and round. "Isn't there something in the Bible about *fatted calves?*" he wondered "And I'm not even religious."

All the while he was selling the desk, pointing out the fine French walnut, the contoured, beveled top and carved serpentine façade—John gloried in the details of the stories he told to Lena, the way she ate them up—it was all he could do to look Mrs. Chestnut in the eye, to avoid glancing down at the white toilet paper in the shadows behind her, which was waving its arms, shouting, *look at me, look at me!* Walking back toward his desk, following her, staring at the tail of toilet paper, urgency grabbed him by the shoulders.

Any second now, she might feel it tickle her fatted calf. Then what, when she realized it was there? That he had seen it all along, and said nothing? Forget that sale. Finally, boldly, he made his move: nimbly—*I'm pretty light on my feet for a big guy*—planting his toe on the paper, which came floating to the floor, and he hustled up close behind her, before she could turn around and bear witness to her shame.

"Didn't she feel it?" Lena asked.

"I don't think so. Her shoulders kind of shivered a little, though."

"That poor lady."

"Oh, I don't know. She never knew. She'll never know—I spared her the shame."

"So—did she buy it?"

"She said she'd have to think about it. There was a piece at Bish's she wanted to look at again." With the utterance of *Bish* came a sour turn of lip.

"The old bag. You should have stuffed the toilet paper back up her dress."

"Up her dress? I should have wrapped her in it like a mummy."

Mrs. Chestnut as a toilet-paper-mummified Elmer Fudd nearly caused another champagne geyser, and when the giggling was over, when the cheese and crackers and pepperoni were gone, they made love again. Afterward they cuddled, John too anxious to nap—he had to be home before eleven, when Alice got out of work. He stared at the pleated red drapes, at the picture on the wall of a waterfall that seemed to be defying gravity, falling on a slant.

Finally, when it was time, he rolled over, reached for the bottle, poured the last drops into their glasses, and proposed a toast: "To another ten years."

No laugh this time, no smile. Somber, sober Lena. Sudden mood swing, sudden exhaustion. An oddly maternal look on her face, she leaned up and kissed his cheek, ran her fingers over it. "Your beard needs a trim," she said.

Your beard needs a trim, your beard needs a trim, he thought, and thought—but no, it was definitely not one of their punch lines. And then Lena told him she'd been to the doctor that day. She told him they were running tests. She told him not to worry.

Later, when he told Alice about Mrs. Chestnut and the toilet paper, it laid an egg. "I don't see how that could happen," Alice said. "You use the toilet paper, you drop it in the toilet. How could you have any hanging out? What was it hanging out of? Her butt? Her underwear?" This was why he seldom told her his stories.

"You know, I never thought to ask her," might have come out a little too harshly.

Alice said, "Well, I just don't see how it could happen."

Did she think he was making it up? He didn't ask. He was still thinking about Lena, about her trip to the doctor's. What tests? He said, "I guess you had to be there."

"I guess," Alice said, "if you say so."

"Did you ever notice how much she looks like Elmer Fudd?" One last try.

"Who? Mrs. Chestnut?"

"I didn't think so."

She gave him a frown halfway between puzzled and annoyed. She was tired, just home from work; John had beat her home by twenty minutes, paid the sitter and sent her home. Alice asked if Georgie was asleep, and John said he was. Georgie was five now. Alice sat on the sofa across from John in her nurse's whites, and they stared at the news for a while. She pulled off her shoes, put her ankle on her knee and started rubbing her foot, long toes, a farmer's daughter's toes. A Freedom Riders bus had been bombed in Alabama, a Little Leaguer killed in California, hit in the heart by a pitch. What a world. What, he wondered, did these two things have to do with Lena's medical tests and with Alice sitting here unhappy, longsuffering, probing for hope in her foot? There was a time when he had rubbed her feet for her, even though sometimes they were sweaty, even a little smelly, and he wasn't sad when that old custom fell by the wayside. She didn't ask anymore. He didn't offer.

"I wonder if you'd have thought that story was funny," he said, "if *Raymond* had told it to you." John hadn't brought Raymond up in years.

Alice looked puzzled.

A crash and clatter from the kitchen—they looked at each other with synchronized sighs. Georgie again. Their son, the sleepwalker.

He'd slipped down the stairs and into the kitchen, his destination of choice when he sleepwalked. They'd never heard him over the news. John switched on the overhead light and there he was, Superman pajamas, cookie jar under his arm, lid broken on the floor, stuffing Oreos into his mouth that was black around the edges. His eyes closed. If he moved he might step on a jagged shard. John picked him up, Alice headed for the broom in the corner. Georgie kept munching. He was heavy for five, a hefty load.

Roly Poly, daddy's little fatty, bet he's gonna be a man someday.

John hated that song. But he loved his boy, the best that he could.

"That is funny," Edna said about Mrs. Chestnut and the toilet paper, though you'd never have known it by the way she said it. Perhaps it was just the cold light of morning, perhaps the serial retelling, but John had to admit to himself that it didn't seem as funny now. "Good one," Edna added for good measure. Another quiet sip of coffee.

"Good one? That's the best you can do? I almost shit my pants. Hey, come to think of it—you don't suppose that's what happened to her?"

"It's awful early," Edna said. "My funny bone's still asleep."

The back door was open and the morning sun slanted in across the yellow linoleum of Edna's kitchen floor, bringing with it the scent of pine trees and dewy grass, the memory of Chuckie crying. Edna had always been a morning person, but now, if John showed up before nine, it seemed to bother her. Now that she was retired she wanted to sleep in, she said, now that she was getting older she needed her beauty rest, but anytime he ignored her advice and showed up earlier, she was always up and about, on her third cup of coffee at least.

He had a feeling, still, again, that Edna knew something he didn't. The nature of mothers, he supposed, the feeling he'd had all his life. He remembered the astonishment he'd felt when she'd told him—he was maybe twenty-one, just going into the army—that she'd known all along the real reason he never wanted her to cut all his fingernails when he was little. He'd always insisted she leave one long, the better to scratch with, he'd said. But Edna revealed she'd always known it was to pick his nose. Now, this morning in her kitchen with sunlight and pine scent, it was déjà vu all over again, Edna the Great and Powerful.

"I think you should tell that one to Phil. He'd get a big kick out of it."

Bish. John's lip curled. "My buddy Phil? My close pal and good friend Phil?"

"You know, what is it you have against that man, anyway?"

What did he *have* against that man? What *did* he have against him?

Lena, medical tests, rumbled through his mind and out the other side. The abruptness of the question caught him by surprise. Bish was a business rival, of course. He stole sales from him. John's shop, Northey's Antiques, was in a converted filling station on the west end of Main, the end less traveled, near the Presbyterian Church, a funeral parlor and a few offices. If you ever needed a tooth filled while having your will made out, your car insured or your body embalmed, John's end of Main was the place to go. If, on the other hand, you needed to pick up aspirin or a candy bar, Bish's place, Forget-Me-Nots, was on the other end of Main, along with Sandt's Drug Store, the Five and Ten, the Western Auto, a jeweler, a florist, you name it, across from the Court House, near Jum's, where all the traffic was, all the potential customers. That's what he had against him. That and a grudge about a stolen tea table. That he himself had stolen. But shouldn't Phil have warned him off, asked him if he'd looked into the provenance of the piece? Shouldn't he have? That's what he had against him. He supposed. There must be more.

"You name it," John said. But his heart wasn't really in it.

After he left Edna's, he headed down toward Main, toward Forget-Me-Nots. A good business plan called for a proactive approach, Bish had taught him that years ago, and John thought it would be good to see for himself the piece Mrs. Chestnut had described, the piece Bish was willing to let go for less than John wanted for the Provencal desk. This is what he told himself. But somehow, for some reason, he also couldn't help but wonder if Phil Bish mightn't find Mrs. Chestnut's toilet paper tail as hilarious as he and Lena

had. In the old days they'd have shared a good laugh about
it, of that John was certain.

What *did* he have against that man, anyway?

The front of Forget-Me-Nots, an old store front, was
filled with light. Ladies' apparel had been sold there at one
time, long ago; John could remember looking through the
window at the women's underwear when he was a kid. It
took him a minute to spot Bish in the shadows by a cluttered
shelf of porcelain collectibles, eyeing John like a mama bear
with a cave full of cubs. The back of the place was poorly
lit, as Bish had always been a thrifty man, and on cloudy
days it was entirely gloomy, on sunny days, like this one, it
was schizophrenic. John ran his finger over a table top where
half a dozen Register clocks were sitting, leaving a trail in
the dust.

"What do you want, John?" Bish said.

An excellent question. What did he want? "Just
browsing, thank you."

Bish nearly smiled. It wasn't easy for him not to, as he'd
been smiling at customers, and at everybody else in general,
for close to seventy years. He was tall, thin and bald, shaped
like a big cigar. John remembered blowing bubbles through
his straw into his Coke when he was little, at the Eagles,
glancing up to see Phil Bish and his mother dancing, or, their
dance interrupted as they both threw back their heads to
laugh at something, Phil's joke, Edna's joke, the horrible
music of the band. The puzzled look on the faces of his father
and Mrs. Bish, Millie, frozen, a snapshot in his memory.
"Please—let me know if I can help you in any way," Bish
said, and John was this close to telling him the Mrs. Chestnut
anecdote, when who should waddle through the clattering
front door but the devil herself, small world.

Seeing John, Mrs. Chestnut froze in her tracks, her face
faltering into a frown. She looked at Phil, then back at John,

than Phil again. She said, "Oh, dear," and turned and walked out, leaving them there, alone, two big men looking at one another and the empty doorway, an unlikely pair of broken-hearted suitors.

Alone in his shop, Lena on the phone, fifty miles away in her own lonely shop, she told him they thought it was breast cancer.

The silence after was a roar in his head.

Cancer in those days meant dead. 1961.

"Are they sure?"

"How the hell can I get breast cancer?" She was angry. "In these little things? I could see if I had a rack like . . . like . . ."

"Like Mrs. Chestnut?" he said helpfully.

She laughed or sobbed, or both. They'd joked about her little boobs before. Whenever the subject of size came up, D-cup, C-cup or B-cup, she'd always maintained that her size was tea-cup. "Bad things come in small packages," she said.

The May sunshine was cold and sterile, contrary to everything God intended May to be, but then everything on the drive to Cranberry, the drive he'd made hundreds of times before, was foreign and unfamiliar, including his own heartbeat, which he couldn't chase out of his throat. He counted cows for a while to avoid thinking, but there was no fun in that without Georgie in the backseat, without the heat of cow-counting competition. How Georgie cried, actual tears, when they passed a graveyard on his side and he lost all his cows (the rules of the game), and John felt tears in his own eyes, no graveyard in sight, just Lena's little boobs, and the sight of her walking away with another man. Two or three years after he met her, Lena had dated for a while. She was open about it—he was married, why shouldn't she date?—and once, a miscommunication, John had arrived just before Vincent, the man she was seeing. John (Lena introduced him to Vincent as an old friend) watched them walk out the door, watched her walk away across the yard to his car, watched Vincent put his arm around her, snow flurries in the air, Christmas music on the radio, and it was all he could do not to cry.

In a field he witnessed a little cow chasing its mother, a little calf, Mrs. Chestnut and her fatted calves, the toilet paper trailing, Lena laughing, the *Closed* sign in the window of his shop, middle of the day. You *must* keep regular hours, so your customer can depend on you to be there when you say you'll be: the Gospel according to Bish. No matter, not today. Should Alice, Edna, any of his friends or customers, ask where'd he'd been, he'd say simply that he'd gotten bored and decided to treat himself to a movie at the Harmony Mills Mall. After ten years of living a double life, John had developed an expertise in easy deception. Or maybe today he would tell them his lover was grievously ill and he'd gone to her. Maybe today he just didn't care. Maybe.

"My Aunt Dorothy had it," Lena said, her pale skin too small for her face. "She had a radical mastectomy. That's what they call it when they cut off your boobs, John."

A little booger hanging from the front of her nostril troubled him. It was not the kind of thing easily mentioned in the course of a conversation such as this, so John reached over and snatched it, and she said *ouch* and juked back. "You had something on your nose," he said. She frowned at him. "I love you," he said.

"Yeah, right," she said. "What, a booger?"

He'd wanted to hold her, to comfort her, to say something noble and uplifting, words to give her hope. Instead he'd snatched a booger from her nose. The rickety kitchen chair gave a squawk beneath his bulk. In the window, the bluebird light-catcher refused to catch light, the sun behind a cloud. "I'm hungry," he said. "Want to get something to eat?"

"Haven't you been listening?" she said. "The biopsy results came back."

His stomach growled, as though it were talking back. "I'm sorry," he said, but whether he was apologizing for his stomach talking back, or for not listening, or for being hungry, or for the biopsy results coming back, he couldn't be sure. Neither could she. He said, "I love you," again when she didn't say anything else.

She made a fist. Her face was a fist that looked away, toward the bluebird that refused to shine, then up to her mud-colored cupboards. "Yeah, right," she said.

"So tell me again about Raymond," said John, lying in ambush when Alice got home. Khrushchev was on the news. John turned the volume off. He wanted a confession. Things were different now. Now, with Alice's confession, he could go to Lena. Lena needed him now. Raymond had gone from a golden key to unlock the door to a sledge hammer to batter it down.

"Where were you this afternoon?" she said. "The shop was closed."

"I had things I had to do. I went to a movie."

"You had things you had to do? So you went to a movie?"

"Wait a minute. Don't change the subject. I asked you about this Raymond character."

The ambush had failed. Almost as if she'd known, had been waiting for it, waiting for it for years. The wild, frightened look in her doe eyes retreated behind the barricades, and she stared at him with something like resolve. Over the last ten years she'd held the hand of many a dying person. "Yes, you did. Again. And I asked you where you were today."

"I was bored. There were no customers. I started thinking, again, about this Raymond. It was just me and him, so I left, I went to a movie, I thought maybe that would help, but it didn't. I realized the only thing that will help is for you to tell me what really happened."

She stared at him for a second. On the television a home run was hit. "After ten years?"

"Is there a statute of limitations on infidelity?"

Again she stared. Almost as if she knew about him and Lena, knew what an incredibly hypocritical fraud he was. "I told you before, we were friends. We hit it off. We got along. He would actually sit down and talk to me. We had real conversations. He knew how to talk to people—there was nobody else around here for me to talk to then, remember? I was all alone. You left me here all alone while you were off somewhere doing God-knows-what."

"Just how friendly were you? I heard he spent the night."

"We were friends. He was pleasant. He was a good nurse. He knew how to treat a lady."

"Raymond knew how to treat a lady? In the biblical sense?"

"Yes! Raymond knew how to treat a lady! Yes! I slept with him once!"

A staggering silence of momentous proportions. A face talking without words on the television. John was stunned, dizzy, unsure of what to do with the hot golden nugget that had fallen into his hand.

"I fixed the lid," came a voice out of nowhere.

Georgie. He'd snuck down the stairs again, hid behind the couch—he wasn't sleepwalking this time. He walked around, an object in his hands, the lid from the cookie jar, which he handed to John as though it were no big deal, as though he heroically mended broken cookie jar lids every day. He climbed up in his Superman pajamas, between them, his mother, his father, cheeks chubby and red. "Mommy helped me," he said, almost like a question.

John was surprised when he woke up on the sofa, not because he was on the sofa, but because he had slept. Apparently soundly, for a number of hours, as the living room was bright as mid-day. No one else was up. He wondered if Lena was up yet. What did she even do in the morning, he wondered. Alone. No him to be seen. At the table in the breakfast nook, sun slanting in, her elbows on the table. Lonely? Cupping her cup in her hands. Legs crossed at the knees, foot idly swinging—the same way she sat after lunch, after dinner, any time they had the chance to share a meal, lingering afterwards, lingering as long as they could, because God knew when they'd have the chance to see each other again. Sipping her coffee, staring at her bluebird, cupping her boob in her hand, squeezing the lump. How could he have missed it? The lump. Was she thinking about him? Wondering what he was doing fifty miles away, with Alice?

Tiptoeing, he looked in on Alice still in bed, pretending to sleep. He looked in on Georgie. A five-year-old, sound asleep, twitching, fists flailing, muttering in a restless dream.

Sitting on the sofa, he listened to the quiet. He looked at the shadows in the empty corner where Fauntleroy, the old dog, had slept so long ago. Fauntleroy had died to make room for Georgie. He looked in the shadows for something to despise about his wife, but all he could find there were all the things that she should despise about him. The fraud. The liar. The coward.

He turned to his mother, as he usually did. Halfway up Valley Street, even before he got there, he sensed danger, as though he were clinging to the side of a cliff, about to lose his grip, and this was even before he turned onto Oak and saw the flashing lights. The laurel was about to blossom, shrubs leafing out nicely, glistening in the morning May sunshine, and there was the ambulance, gaudy and glittering, in front of Edna's. John pulled up, got out, sniffed the scent of pine, saw Chuckie and the neighborhood kids, hurried to where Edna was standing at the bottom of the stairs. Her arms were crossed, her hair tied back in a red bandana. "What happened?" he said. "What's going on?"

She looked up at him from under her sad, damp lashes. "Shut up," she growled.

Two ambulance attendants—he recognized Harold Bunker—wrestled the gurney down the narrow stairs. The man strapped to it, face gray as a ghost under an oxygen mask, was Phil Bish.

Phil Bish died that day in his mother's bed. He was DOA when they got him to the hospital at the top of the hill. He was DOA at the bottom of Edna's stairs, but they didn't know it then.

Lena out-lived him by only two years.

He remembered the green of the overcast day in late May when he left her, looking for the owl on the way to his car, the fat green leaves of the maples and elms, the shrubbery, the laurel and rhododendron, all so brilliant in the diffused, diminished light. He remembered being suffocated by the light, dark, lemon, lime, apple, rich, thick, luxurious shades of green. By the accusation.

REITZ & RITUALS

After the game, Jerry invited his teammates up to his place to celebrate their win. Sterck's had outlasted Proud Judy's 10 – 9, securing second place, which meant a spot in the playoffs; last year they'd missed out by a mere two games. This year, 1967, was only the second of the league's existence, and enthusiasm still ran high. Outside of the bars and the Moonlight Drive-in, where the movies changed maybe once every two weeks, there was little else to do on Hartsgrove's sultry summer evenings, and it would take another eleven years, when the youth of the men of Sterck's Terriers was already beginning to slip away, before enthusiasm for the Men's Slow Pitch Softball League had waned to the point where the league petered out.

The Reitzes, Jerry and his wife Gloria, lived in a new stone house on a deep, wooded, hillside lot. It was somewhat elegant—*ritzy*, as in "Reitz's ritzy place," as Chuck, the shortstop and one of the guests that evening, liked to put it—and the deck in back afforded a view of

Hartsgrove's hillsides and a portion of Main Street, the brick facades, replica gas streetlamps and the high, lighted dome of the courthouse. Chuck and his teammates (and their wives and girlfriends, few of whom were not in attendance at every game) liked to gather at the Reitz's when the invitation was offered, as it seemed a more sophisticated, a *cleaner*, gathering place than Jum's or the Chug-a-lug Tavern, or one of the other dim and dreary Hartsgrove bars in which to celebrate their victories, brood over their losses, take stock of their lives at that time and place.

The games were played under the lights on a new field down at the bottom of the town where the three creeks converged, and on this hot evening in late August, the night air was still and heavy, and the view from the deck, the yellowish hue of the streetlamps on Main, resembled an old photograph. They sat on the deck, the view there for the taking, and they talked and listened to *Sgt Pepper's Lonely Hearts Club Band* from Jerry's new stereo, turned up loud enough for the sound to carry outside. Looking back later, he couldn't remember mosquitoes. Over the years, mosquitoes had become a worry, but Jerry didn't remember them then, that night in particular as they sat outside in the open air, like many other nights, and he wondered if it was their sweat, their youth, that repelled them, or was it before mosquitoes had invaded Hartsgrove, before they'd discovered the place on the map? The men, his teammates, wore their Sterck's uniforms, garish gold jerseys with black letters and numerals—Jerry's was 21, Roberto Clemente's number—and gold pants with broad, black, vertical stripes, and sat out on the deck with cans and bottles of beer in hand, each with his own favorite brand, Iron City, Budweiser, Duquesne, Rolling Rock, having stopped on the way to purchase their own preferred six-packs. They sat on the deck railing, on the cooler, in chairs around the patio table, on the floor of the deck itself. They talked about the game—Jerry, not normally the strongest of hitters, had managed to drive in the tie-breaking run with a bloop single over second—and about the Pirates' so-so season, hovering around .500 (the magical season of '60, when the Bucs, against all odds, had defeated the mighty Yankees in the Series, was still vivid in their memories), and they talked about Dean Chance's second no-hitter of the month for the Twins. The women, the wives and girlfriends, congregated for the most part at the other end of the deck, at the picnic table and on chairs brought out from the kitchen, having their own conversations, quieter than the men, less boisterous and celebratory, discussing childcare and childbirth—Bucky's wife, Brenda, had just learned she was pregnant—and parents and jobs and boyfriends and husbands. For a long while they considered what Billie Joe McAllister and the girl in the song might have thrown off the Tallahatchie Bridge: a baby? A wedding ring? A draft card? Missy, who liked to think outside the box, speculated it was a note in a bottle: *Help! Rednecks are holding me hostage and I can't escape!* Cathy, Jerry's and Gloria's little girl, six at the time and the only child present, spent the evening enjoying her unique status while nevertheless longing for someone to play with. She alternated between her dad's lap, her mother's, and the bowls of chips and cheese doodles on the table. Now and then she danced by herself to the music. At every opportunity, Gloria wiped her little girl's mouth and hands, golden and greasy from cheese doodles, and made her straighten her back. Cathy had the same long, elegant spine that Gloria had also inherited from her mother, but the child was determined to slouch. Gloria tried to remember if she'd slouched at that age, concluding that most likely she had not. "You are such a mess," she chided her little girl, "Mommy's little mess." Gradually, over the next hour or two, the alcohol did its work, the men and women intermingling more, and some drifted off, back to their own homes and lives, until only a few couples remained, lounging on the deck, taking in the music and the conversation and the view of their town down below, pinned into place by inertia and contentment, by the heavy air of the Hartsgrove night.

Missy was the wild card. Or, the more Jerry thought about it, the time bomb. She had a reputation as something of a wild woman, and here she was, sitting quietly chatting (albeit drinking like a sailor) with a quiet group of friends. Missy was the only one who had not been to the game, for she was not married to one of the team members, nor to anyone else. She'd arrived with Denny, the only teammate whose wife had not been there. Denny had stopped at Jum's to purchase his six-pack of Duquesne, finding Missy there drinking, feeding dimes to the juke box, bored and restless, amenable to a new scene. Denny had puffy eyes behind thick glasses, he had fantasies about Missy, and he envied the hippies in San Francisco, letting his dark blond hair go long; not too long, however, as Mr. Matson, his boss at Matson Lumber where he was in sales, would not tolerate much length. Jerry observed Missy and his wife from across the deck, fascinated by their apparent rapport: he hadn't heard the joke, but once Missy and Gloria had erupted with laughter, clasping each other's arms, touching their foreheads together. True, they'd known each other for years, having been introduced at the Country Club when Gloria was a toddler, Missy a little older. Their parents were among Hartsgrove's upper crust: Missy's father was a judge now, having been the county sheriff for years before that. Gloria's father was a shrewd and wealthy businessman for whom

Jerry worked at his company, Zimmerman's Gas and Coal, and her mother, who'd worked for a time with Missy's father when he was sheriff, was still politically active. But around the time adolescence had set in, Gloria's and Missy's paths had parted, a high road and a low.

Jerry broke free of his languid captivity and went inside to restart the record, which had ended. The noise felt necessary. He didn't like the lulls in the conversation when the sound of the occasional truck groaning up the East Main Street hill made him feel somehow precarious. He watched for a while through the window from the darkened living room the young men in black and gold tribal attire, young women with painted faces and lengthy lashes, all perched in place on this precarious social web. Jerry looked down at his own uniform, an effective and comfortable disguise, and he shifted his feet, placing his hands on his hips. He was a good-looking man with dark, curly hair and a charming grin he knew how to employ, and women had always seemed attracted to him, though he could never be certain if the attraction was honest, or if they were conspiring to cast him as a clown. He took a deep, resigned breath that quavered its way in. Outside, in the middle of the deck, his little girl took a heaping handful of cheese doodles. Only he, unseen, was watching her. She wandered to the steps of the deck, tilting her head to take in the view of Main Street down below, as she methodically, mechanically, placed cheese doodle after cheese doodle in her mouth, one at a time, savoring: cheese doodle heaven! It occurred to him how indebted he was to that frail creature, his daughter, Ben Zimmerman's daughter's daughter, how secure she made him feel, for Ben Zimmerman was absolutely wild about her, his only granddaughter. She climbed on her mother's lap, and Gloria took a napkin to the girl's face, wiping hard, as if trying to eradicate her lips. Cathy freed herself and went to Missy, who embraced her with a smile, and Jerry's knees went weak at the sight, as though everything the world had to offer was unfurling itself before him like a meadow in the morning sun.

When Jerry came back outside, Gloria went in. She'd been awaiting his return impatiently, as she didn't feel it proper to leave their guests with neither host nor hostess. She needed another glass of Chablis—she hadn't offered her wine around, as perhaps a good hostess should, for her guests, her so-called guests, all seemed quite content sucking on their cans and bottles—and she needed her nail file: damned picnic tables. A deck was not her idea of the best place to entertain, although for this particular crowd, she was perfectly content with it. Jerry's "teammates." Ever since high school, even before, whenever she gazed upon the short one, Chuck, his wide, grinning face, all she could see was a monkey. She was not particularly proud of the feeling, but she couldn't deny it either. She tried to like him, she tried to like all Jerry's friends, but Chuck was thick and dull, and Denny was not much better, just as thick, just as dull, perhaps a bit less insufferable. Bucky was the only one with an upside; at least he had the sense to keep his mouth shut for the most part and offer a facade of mystery, of allure. And don't get her started on the women—even her friend Missy, for whom, at least, there was hope, provided she could manage to outgrow this infantile phase she was passing through and embrace the grown-up world. It wasn't easy, smiling, being civil, but it was an obligation.

   She filed her nail, then touched it up with polish, purple polish, not a perfect match for the polish that Sadie had applied when Sadie had done her nails on Wednesday, but close enough for a dark evening on a deck. For present company. She stood before her mirror in the master bathroom, watching herself blow on the tip of her finger, her black hair sweeping back from her forehead in elegant waves, her dark eyes bold and gritty. Conversations from the deck drifted in, the occasional guffaw and monkey laugh, and Gloria let the sounds buoy her up, like bubbles rising up all around her in the pool, till she was floating on the surface, above it all. Then she heard the television in the living room, the low, earnest voice of the announcer on the eleven o'clock news. Where were the riots this time? Leaving the bathroom, she peeked in: a burning car, black, angry men running, smashing. Detroit still? Memphis? Earlier in the month it had been Newark. Gloria found her breath going shallow as she stared at the news, bad news, far away from Hartsgrove where not a single black family lived, but still it seemed too near. *Unrest* they called it, a nice, civil word, a nice, civil lie; a revolution was what it was, a civil war. She'd read a letter in Life magazine from a woman—presumably a black woman—saying that black people do not desire a reconciliation with whites, that they would prefer "all-out war." Gloria decided that she would bring it up outside, see if there was any way she could coax a serious discussion of current events out of her husband's guests, see if they could rise above batting averages, pop songs, beer and motherhood. She'd discussed the riots with Jerry. She couldn't understand it. After all, hadn't they won their civil rights, wasn't progress being made? What, exactly, did they want now? But Jerry had made light of it, made light of her, telling her parents that Gloria was afraid a black man was going to ravage her and loot her crystal collection. Jerry could be a bastard.

The kitchen was dark, but for the splash of light when she opened the refrigerator. She poured her wine, then stood in the dark looking out at the deck through the window, at the young people gathered there, calm and uncoiled, not a care in the world. She tapped her purple nails on the tile counter-top, tap-tap-tapping in an urgent inner rhythm that was quite out of sync with the mournful voice of John Lennon from the den, *I heard the news today, oh boy . . . four thousand holes in Blackburn, Lancashire . . .*

Fed up with the Beatles—*Sgt Pepper's* was on an endless cycle—Chuck the shortstop went inside and changed the record, without being asked, without asking permission. He was a short man, a stature befitting a shortstop, as his teammates kiddingly observed, with a barrel chest (albeit a smallish barrel) and a bristling black flattop, one of the few such haircuts remaining on the Sterck's Terriers, or anywhere else around town. Chuck never cared much for the Beatles, certainly not for their newer music which was even more removed from his beloved rock and roll and simple ballads, and he'd never have listened to *Sgt Pepper's* of his own volition; he disliked the album cover, and perversely enjoyed admitting that yes, yes indeed, he did judge the album by its cover. He hated anything the least bit psychedelic or remotely hippie; he'd been eyeing Denny's lengthening hair with distaste. Spying an album of the '50's greatest hits, he put it on the turntable and lowered the needle. The old-time music—the power of those songs, how they moved him about in time and place! "Love Letters in the Sand" beamed him instantly to the sock hop in the Tastee Freeze parking lot the night they were seniors when Gloria had stepped on a shard of broken glass.

The song transported Gloria there as well. How broken glass could have materialized on the pavement of the parking lot, pavement that had been swept clean and carefully inspected in anticipation of the evening's sock hop—a *sock* hop, for God's sake!—was a mystery, and while malicious intent had been suspected, it was a mystery that would never be solved. Gloria frowned. "Who put this on?"

Chuck hesitated at the tone of her voice. Bucky raised his hand in apparent confession. He raised it not eagerly, like a student who knows the answer, but slowly, coolly, noticeably; everything Bucky did was cool and conspicuous. Seven years before, when most of them were away at college, Bucky's girlfriend, a senior at Hartsgrove High, had been killed by the janitor. Ever since, an aura of heroic tragedy had clung to him like a cape, his dark and brooding good looks, his sleepy hooded eyes, only enhancing the effect. His wife, Brenda, waif-like and devoted (even more so now, in the early stages of pregnancy) seemed to never want to relinquish contact with him, as if the same could happen to him, as if, having been exposed, he might be susceptible now.

Bucky slowly twisted his pointing finger toward Chuck. "The shortstop did it."

"You got something against nostalgia?" Chuck asked the gathering at large.

"Enough Beatles for pity's sake," said his wife, Sally, a tomboy poised with ankle on knee. Her hair was the color of weak tea.

" 'Love Letters in the Sand' always reminds me of the sock hop that night you cut your foot," said Chuck, grinning. The song was nearly over by now.

"Me too," Gloria said. "Which is why I detest it." The song was not all she detested; there, the monkey grin again. Instinctively, she reached for her little girl, but "Jailhouse Rock" came on, and Missy took Cathy by the hands and began to jitterbug with her, there on the deck in their midst. Missy felt that something was expected of her, knew that all the men were watching, waiting; and though she failed to notice, or care, if the women were as well, she felt it was her duty to stand up and be noticed.

Cathy was delighted. The little girl giggled through her clumsy moves as Missy led her through this twirl and that,

that step and this, ignoring the scorn on her mother's face. Watching his daughter, watching Missy, smiling obliquely, Jerry said to his wife, "Wasn't that the night you put a ding in your old man's fender? The same night you cut your foot?"

Gloria raised her eyebrows and pursed her lips. "How would you know? You weren't even there—I was with Al Galbreath that night."

"No, no—that was one of our first dates."

Argument ensued. Chuck thought he remembered that Jerry was there that night, as did his wife, Sally, while Denny admitted he couldn't be sure. Brenda couldn't say, as she didn't think she'd been there herself. She didn't think she'd gone to a single sock hop that whole summer.

"What does it matter?" said Bucky. "Doesn't make any difference if you remember it from being there, or from hearing about it, or from going to other ones just like it. For all intents and purposes, you're talking about exactly the same thing." Bucky had taken philosophy courses at Slippery Rock.

"How so?" said Gloria.

Denny asked if he could borrow one of Jerry's Buds, as his Dukes were all gone.

"I can see that night in my mind just as well as anybody," Bucky said, "and I wasn't there. I've heard about it. I went to other sock hops. I can imagine it. I can see the Tastee Freeze sign, I can see the stars, the kids dancing, I can hear the music—I can even see Gloria stepping on the glass and grabbing her foot and hopping. What's the difference if it's a real memory, or not? At this point in time, it makes absolutely no difference—they're identical."

"Actually I sat down," Gloria said. "I didn't hop."

"But if you weren't really there," Jerry said, "it isn't authentic. It isn't real."

"*Authentic?*" said Bucky. "*Real?* Either way it's only in your mind now, ten years later—it's only chemicals either way."

"I see what you're saying," said Brenda. "I wasn't there either—at least I don't think I was—but in my mind I can see it just like I was."

"What the hell does it matter?" Denny said. "Who cares anyway?"

"I care," Gloria said. "I care very deeply."

"Oh my God," cried Sally, "a bug flew up my nose!"

"A real bug?" Chuck said. His wife jumped to her feet, pressing one nostril shut, blowing hard through the other, hopping as she did so, a war dance of sorts. For a few seconds they watched her stomp and prance, till the bug was successfully expelled, along with a certain amount of mucus. She wiped it away with the back of her hand, looking sheepishly at the staring faces. "What?" she said. "A bug flew up my nose!"

"I don't think I've ever loved you more than I do at this moment," said Chuck.

"Me too," said Denny.

"Ugh," Gloria said. "I think I'm going to have to mop the deck."

"*Swab* the deck," corrected Bucky.

"For Pete's sake," said Sally, taking a napkin and wiping her hand, then wiping the floor at her feet. "It's only a little bit."

"What's a little snot among friends?" said Brenda.

"Jailhouse Rock" having ended, her dance over, Cathy was standing wide-eyed, still holding Missy's hand, staring from one grown-up face to the next, then to the glistening spot on the plank of the deck, where the residual snot still shone. Gloria said, "It's your bedtime little girl," and Cathy sighed, going tragically limp, a dagger piercing her six-year-old heart.

Gloria put her child to bed and Jerry lowered the music, replacing the '50's hits with the Rolling Stones while he was at it. On the deck, the volume was lower as well, separate, quieter conversations replacing the general group chatter. The jitterbug and nose-bug had been the climax, apparently, of the evening. Sally told Bucky and Brenda about a book she'd just finished reading, a real pot-boiler, *Rosemary's Baby.* "Really?" said Bucky, who'd read the book as well, but had kept it to himself. "You want to talk about the spawn of Satan?" he said, and Sally apologized, having forgotten, she said, that Brenda was pregnant (a lie). Missy observed that it might be handy if the little rascal had a tail after all, something to grab when he misbehaved, and Brenda said, "You guys aren't very funny." She was not at all surprised that Sally had brought up the book, as she'd always known, since second grade on the Northside Elementary playground when Sally had pushed her on the swing, kept pushing her higher, wouldn't let her slow down and get off despite her pleas, that Sally was a bully. Unbeknownst to Sally, meanwhile, her husband, Chuck, was telling Jerry about Sally's inability to have a baby, having been born with what the doctor called "tubal abnormalities," something they'd learned only recently, something that even her own parents didn't know, and something she'd never have believed her husband would tell anyone, not even his closest friend, which Jerry was not. Something that even Chuck didn't know had come as good news to Sally, a relief, something Chuck believed she thought was just as tragic and sad as he did.

After the Stones were over, Jerry put on something even quieter, a Lettermen album, full of harmony and pathos and melancholy, and Bucky looked at his watch. During a lull, everyone gazing down at the yellow lights of Main Street, listening to the sad old songs, Bucky said, "I guess it's getting late." There was a slow, reluctant stirring. No one wanted to stay, no one wanted to go. The beer was nearly gone, and Gloria watched Jerry begin to gather up the cans and bottles and put them in the paper bag he was bringing around the deck. Missy had an idea. Though it came to her suddenly, a chick bursting out of an egg, she'd been sitting on it, hatching it, for quite some time without realizing it. She said, "Let's do something."

"Like what?" said Denny.

"Let's go skinny-dipping—I feel like taking my clothes off." It was perfect. It was exactly how she felt.

"Where?" said Denny.

There was a brittle moment of silence, a crackling in the air.

"The dam?" said Chuck.

"I just want to get naked in water," Missy said. "I don't want to get eaten by a bear." Out by the waterworks, the dam was dark, deep in the woods.

"'The Grizzly Bear is huge and wild,'" said Bucky, who'd also taken English at Slippery Rock, and seldom missed a bear cue, "'He has devoured the infant child—'"

"'The infant child is unaware it has been eaten by the bear,'" Brenda said in a ho-hum sing-song. She'd heard the quote from her husband a dozen times before.

"There's a nice, civilized pool out at the Country Club," said Jerry with a shrug.

Gloria glared at her husband. Was she the only one who believed Missy's suggestion was sheer folly? In the background, the Lettermen droned on, superfluous now, unheard. There was new life on the erstwhile bored and drowsy faces, Gloria saw, an aura of restrained excitement. Missy's and Denny's faces were particularly alive with it, though it was not absent from a single face, including her husband's. She drummed her purple nails on the table.

"I like that idea," Missy said of the Country Club.

"Is anyone a member?" said Denny.

"I think after midnight it's open to everyone," said Bucky. "Completely egalitarian."

"I don't know," Brenda whispered to Bucky. "In my condition . . ."

"Oh for heaven's sakes, let's just *go*," Missy said. "Quit *thinking* about it!"

Gloria took a breath, grinding her teeth. She was not opposed to the concept of swimming naked with others for any prudish or sanctimonious reasons. Rather she was less than enthusiastic in this instance simply because of the time and place, the impracticality of the idea, the absence of an immediate pool, for example, and the fact that her little girl was sound asleep in her bed. "It's late," she said, "and we have a little girl upstairs asleep. As enchanting as it sounds, I'm afraid we'll have to pass."

"I don't know," Jerry said, "it sounds like fun. Something different. Something you don't do every day."

"True," said Gloria. "But then you don't go cow-tipping every day, either."

"We can probably scare up a couple of cows to tip on the way out to the Country Club," Chuck said.

The monkey grin again. Gloria's nostrils flared. "Have fun," she said. "I'm going upstairs to check on my daughter."

Jerry was in the mood for adventure. He hated the idea of being left behind. Moreover, he was in the mood to establish that he was not always, despite appearances to the contrary, Gloria's obedient lap dog. "When she said 'have fun,'" he asked of everyone in general, no one in particular, "do you suppose she meant me as well?"

Cathy was dead to the world. Gloria pulled the sheet up to her chin—a sheet was more than enough this warm and humid night—and wiped away a drop of drool, orange in color, at the edge of her daughter's mouth. She heard a car start out front, then another, perhaps another yet. She couldn't tell for certain how many. The sound of the Lettermen from the den ended, the record over, and she listened for whatever the night had to offer, but after the cars had faded away, no other sounds were forthcoming, not a bird, not a breeze, no traffic, nothing but the fragile, barely audible puffs of her little girl breathing. Her own breath she held. A curious chill came over her, despite the heat of the evening, and she had a sensation, not unfamiliar, of vague anticipation, as if she were about to experience a pleasurable thing, a taste perhaps like ice cream, a sound like bells, a delightful bright vista.

What she experienced instead when she went downstairs was isolation. The deck was deserted, stale ashes in ashtrays, beer cans and bottles all about, Jerry's half-full bag abandoned on the floor. They were gone, every one, her husband as well. Someone's forgotten leather mitt hunched beneath the bench like a lurking rat.

The Pine Shadows Country Club was four miles out of town, and the pool was off behind the main building proper, some distance across a deserted parking lot, behind a row of neatly trimmed, low hedges. It was, fortunately and fortuitously, somewhat hidden and therefore well suited for clandestine adventures such as unauthorized swimming of a naked nature. The parking lot remained empty, the intruders having taken the precaution of driving, sans headlights, up the farmer's lane that bordered the back of the golf course, and walking the short distance across the practice greens to the pool. Missy led the way, steadfast and eager, her single-mindedness lending a particularly perverse sense of seriousness to the venture, although Jerry, feeling the more delinquent for having left behind his wife and child, nonetheless felt the need to stifle a childish chuckle.

It was moonless, a star-filled night, faint illumination abetted by the ambient light from the parking lot lamps.

By the pool, they took off their clothes. Garish gold uniforms abandoned in careless heaps on the concrete apron, alongside the light summer dresses of the women. Quickly, they jumped into the water with modest splashes. There they were quiet, dog-paddling about aimlessly, not only out of fear of discovery—for now they were essentially fugitives—but out of awkwardness, out of not knowing what to do next. What do you do once you're naked in the water? Then what?

What was behind the adventure in the first place beyond voyeurism, abstract tantalization? Jerry wondered, perhaps only briefly at the time, but more curiously over the years. The culture of Nudism was foreign to them. No one's cousin was a nudist, no one knew a nudist, no one's cousin knew a nudist. Nor did anyone suspect in his or her wildest dreams (or nightmares) that anything more could possibly come of it, certainly nothing akin to an orgy, and Jerry suspected that no one there that dim night would be bold or brassy or drunk enough to engage in such uninhibited behavior even if it were to somehow try to emerge—Hartsgrove was not Hollywood or New York City, not San Francisco. In the end, voyeurism and tantalization were probably the whole of it. As Denny explained when Jerry brought it up later, in whispers, sitting on the end of the bench watching Chuck at bat against the Golden Dawn Warriors: It was a great chance to see a bunch of women naked.

Missy climbed out of the pool and walked dripping to the diving board, mounted it, stood for a few moments feeling all eyes upon her—she could feel them on her skin. She needed to take charge, to lead, to show that she was utterly unafraid. All her life she'd felt naked and helpless, and she'd learned that her best recourse was to *be* naked and anything *but* helpless. She bounced on the board several times, shoulders back, back straight, her breasts buoyant, then dived into the water. Denny, wide-eyed, speechless, sputtering, splashed and flailed in the deep end, cursing the water on his glasses that impaired his vision. It was wrong not to be able to touch her, it was unfair, it was worse—it was a fundamental assault on justice. Now, more than ever, how he envied the hippies and all he'd read about free love. Free love! "What's your wife going to think?" said Brenda from the middle of the pool where she clung to Bucky as if to stay afloat, and Denny said, "What's your husband going to think?" at which Bucky only lowered his face in the water and glowered at Denny like a crocodile submerged to the eyes. Chuck yelled to Denny, "Don't you usually take off your glasses when you go swimming?" but Denny paid no heed. He was staring again toward Missy, still thinking about free love; love had been anything but free in his experience, having cost him dearly ever since his wife's early pregnancy (at sixteen) the cost escalating, along with her weight, every year. Chuck meanwhile was cracking wise about boobs and goosebumps and not always being able to distinguish one from the other, for the water was chilly despite the warm evening air, and Sally countered with a belittling remark concerning shrinkage. Jerry decided to see how far he could swim in the blackness underwater and pop up again where least expected. He wanted to get away and watch, play an anthropologist on television, witness behavior under stress, and if, along the way, he happened to catch an eyeful or two himself, that was fine too. Missy was climbing out of the water again when the headlights crossed over the dark pool water.

A car came across the parking lot. Missy slipped back into the pool. They watched without a word, still, treading water, nearly motionless, watched the blue Chrysler pull to a stop near the pool.

"Speaking of wives," Brenda said.

"Gloria," said Jerry. His wife got out of the car, walked around the hedges, stood looking down at the bobbing figures. "You people are something," she said.

"Where's Cathy?" said Jerry.

"Sound asleep."

"You left her alone?"

Gloria inhaled sharply. "You must be drunker than I thought. She's in the car. Asleep in the back."

"Oh—do you think she'll stay that way?"

Gloria ignored the question. "You all must be drunker than I thought," she said. "Look at you."

"Come on in, the water's fine," said Missy.

"Take off your clothes!" cried Bucky, of all people. "Take off your damn clothes!"

"No clothes," said Chuck. "Rules are rules."

Staring at Jerry, Gloria unhurriedly unbuttoned her blouse, took it off, folded it neatly. She placed it on the ground, then stared at her husband again as she slowly removed her shorts. Denny in the pool tried to muster up a semblance of a bom-bom-bom stripper's beat, but the effort fell flat, largely ignored, as everyone paddled impatiently, waiting, watching Gloria stare at her husband as she finished undressing. When her bra and panties had topped off her neat little pile, she jumped into the water to a chorus of quiet cheers and made her way to her husband. "Happy, dear?"

Jerry didn't answer right away. The others began to stir, milling and splashing about, Missy climbing from the pool for another dive, Denny as wide-eyed as ever, Chuck dunking his wife's head under water, Sally swimming after him, seeking revenge. Jerry and Gloria floated close, circling one another, predator and prey. Jerry said around mouthfuls of water, "You. Are. Absolutely. Stunning." Gloria smiled obliquely, her eyelids floating.

Take off your damn clothes was what woke Cathy up, a very mysterious awakening indeed, a man's loud voice, and at first she didn't know where she was, until she remembered, quite vaguely (she thought she'd dreamed it) her mommy picking her up, carrying her downstairs and putting her in the back of the car. This was where she was now. She touched the leather to be sure. She found her chewing gum in the ashtray where her mom had made her spit it out before they went in to grandma's. She put the gum back in her mouth, too hard to chew. She sat up and looked all around. It was a big, wide place where the ground was hard and black with lines painted all over it, and some poles with lights on top like streetlights, and a great big house way over. The big house looked familiar. She'd been here, she thought, with her mommy and daddy, to eat, she thought, but it was never like this: where were all the cars, the lights, the people? Where was her blankie? She was scared and began to breathe hard and she realized she had to pee. Splashing noises, someone playing in water. And voices. Close by the car were bushes. From over on the other side of the bushes, where it was very dark, the noises came. Cathy was scared. Where was her mommy? Her daddy? Were they over there? Should she get out of the car? Should she look? What if something was out there? She began to cry, but she had to be quiet.

Something might hear her. Something might get her.

From the pool, Chuck and Denny, then Sally, climbed out and dived off the board, becoming bolder, more immune to inhibition. Bucky and Brenda still clung together floating in the middle, and no one could see Bucky's hands, what they were doing, nor notice in the darkness Brenda's face, and how she held her breath. Jerry and Gloria circled leisurely, watching each other and the others, astonished. Something about the sound of a splash, the water in his ear, something took Jerry back to the cloudy afternoon nearly twenty years before when a boy about twelve, older than Jerry, had dived into the water at the dam, hit a rock and broken his neck, and Jerry thought about the nonchalance of the whole incident, he and his friends only watching in morbid fascination, lost in the gravity, as if they bore witness to tragedies every day. He slapped at the water now, in the midnight pool, swatting at the memory, at his companions, then and now, laughing and playing as if no one was ever going to die.

They heard a little girl crying. Everyone froze in place.

Cathy appeared from behind the hedge, sobbing. "Mommy," she cried. "*Mommy!*" Her face was wet and twisted, arms limp and helpless at her sides. Gloria saw the dark stain where her little girl had peed herself, and was out of the pool quickly, Cathy's eyes going wide at the sight of her naked mother, sobs interrupted. Gloria picked her up, standing by the dark water, rocking, soothing, cooing. Cathy buried her face in the raven-black hair at her mommy's neck, sobs resuming, softer, more like whimpers. Gloria patted her little girl's back, swaying, "There, there . . . it's all right now . . . mommy's here . . . mommy's little Nosy Parker, mommy's little busy-body . . ." Everyone watched. Gloria's tall, nude body, wet and glistening, seemed majestic, regal, to Jerry.

She stooped, clutching her daughter, a feat of strength, taking her clothes with her free hand. Then she walked away, deliberately, naked and elegant, Lady Godiva sans steed.

By the time Cathy had grown up, married, had a baby and become a young widow, the deck behind the house was gone, replaced by a flag-stone patio and an in-ground pool.

The deck was gone and so was Missy, having killed herself in a car accident driving drunk in the late '80s, an accident long overdue, attributable as much to the law of averages as to anything else. What had prompted him to think of Missy this particular afternoon Jerry wasn't sure, but suspected it was a combination of things: the silent isolation of the house as he stood gazing out at the pool through the living room window, the long, beautiful drive up from Morgantown—it was early October and the changing leaves were extraordinary—as well as the fact that this was his first visit home in three weeks. Ordinarily he came home every weekend, simply picking up where he left off, but the extended absence, combined with the emptiness of the place—Gloria hadn't left a note—seemed somehow to trigger the act of remembering, the art of nostalgia.

Home. A schizophrenic concept, but one that had long since grown on him, fitting like an old shoe, ever since he'd quit working for Gloria's father over twenty years before, and had taken a job with Morgan Oil, a competitor, if anything, to Zimmerman's. Jerry's Rebellion. Gloria, of course, as expected, had refused to sell the house or relocate to West Virginia with him, refused to abandon her parents, her home and her life, everything that Jerry wanted to do, although the thought of divorce never entered into the picture. Jerry found an apartment near his job, found another when that house was sold by the landlord and the new owner raised the rent unreasonably (in Jerry's mind), while Gloria maintained their home on the hillside in Hartsgrove and carried on with life as before. Jerry came home every weekend to mow the lawn and fix the leaky faucet. The Reitzes marriage endured.

Where she was this afternoon, this golden autumn afternoon, Jerry didn't know, but he assumed it was a normal errand, the lack of a note notwithstanding. Gloria, despite few overt signs of otherwise aging, was becoming more forgetful. Maybe Ellen, their granddaughter, Cathy's daughter who was five now, had her swimming lesson—the little girl was overweight, albeit adorable, and Gloria and Cathy were forever finding physical activities for the child. He looked on the refrigerator for a schedule, finding none. Since he was there, he opened the door and reached for the bottle of tonic. The sun was shining warmly on the patio, a perfect day for a gin and tonic, perhaps the season's last.

Indian summer. The pool was covered, a chore completed on his last trip home three weeks before, and a scattering of crisp, rust-colored leaves floated here and there in the puddles on the blue pool cover. He sat on a patio chair, gin and tonic on the glass-top table at hand, looking out across the yard and down toward the view of Main— more obscured now by encroaching foliage, less remarkable now in bright daylight amidst the vista of Hartsgrove's brightly colored hillsides. He thought about Missy and the pool, the pool that night at the Country Club, their brief fling with Nudism. Missy had moved away, but had visited her mother in the nursing home frequently (her father, the judge, had passed away well before her mother), and she'd seldom come home without partying. She hadn't aged well. She'd been through two or three husbands, nearing fifty when she died—killed herself—attributable as much, now that Jerry thought about it, to the law of diminishing returns, as to the law of averages. Who had been there that night? Where were the others now? Missy, he thought, was the only one of them who had died, although he wasn't sure about Sally. He'd lost track of her. He'd have to ask Gloria. Chuck and Sally had split up long ago, and Sally had moved to California, he thought, a design consultant for department store windows, or some such profession that seemed to Jerry hardly sustainable. Sally must have had a resourceful side that she'd kept well hidden. Chuck had married another woman and remained childless, and had become a cop, a Hartsgrove policeman, and had arrested Denny, at least twice, for drunken driving. Jerry often saw Chuck in his cruiser, or strutting about in his uniform, shoulders back, smallish barrel chest above a slight paunch now. A natural cop, he'd eventually, after a decade or two, become Chief of the Hartsgrove Police Department, loved by all at last—a success by any measure, Jerry supposed, although he had trouble measuring it as such himself.

Denny had become a bartender. Matson Lumber had long since gone out of business, and he worked at the Golden Steer, wearing his gold vest over his substantial belly, his long hair over his substantial shoulders. Seven kids, Jerry believed, at last count. Bucky had quit teaching at the community college over by Harmony Mills to become a carpenter. Of all of them, Bucky was probably the happiest, he and Brenda still fitting together like the dovetails on the pieces of furniture Bucky lovingly fashioned—for he was more than a carpenter, he was a craftsman, an excellent craftsman at that. He'd made several pieces for the Reitzes, including the cabinets in their remodeled kitchen. Bucky and Brenda were the only ones he and Gloria still saw on a regular basis. Their daughter, the one with whom Brenda had been pregnant that night, had been an uncommonly beautiful child, a tiny birthmark in the shape of a heart at the base of her jaw. Precocious as well, charming and undaunted by adult company, she'd gone to Slippery Rock after her father, and had competed, as Jerry recalled, in the Miss Pennsylvania contest, with some success.

His own little girl, Cathy, had never blossomed into the beauty that her mother had been—or still was, many would argue. Cathy was thicker, less shapely, hair like dirty straw. She'd become a real estate agent, eking out a living, emulating her mother the best she could, not marrying until she was thirty, and then to a large, fat man with no ambition, albeit a loveable, jolly fat man, who'd aimed to please like a St. Bernard. George. He'd had a massive heart attack not long after Ellen was born. Now Cathy was dating a twice-divorced used car salesman, a waste of skin, nearly Jerry's age. Jerry could see visions of his daughter side by side: the little girl in the dark by the pool seeking comfort in the arms of her naked mother, and the grown-up Cathy in the polyester arms of a sleazy man, dancing at the Country Club to the *Tennessee Waltz*. His name was Ernest.

Jerry went inside and made himself another gin and tonic. Giving in to his nostalgia, he found his old *Sgt Pepper's* CD (the vinyl was as long-gone as the deck) and put it on loud enough to hear from the patio. He wondered again where Gloria was. Would she come home and turn off his music?

He felt content, as content as could be expected for a man pushing sixty with a herniated disc, high cholesterol and Y2K bearing down on him, on them all, like the next apocalypse, if the alarmists were to be believed. Morgan Oil was certainly battening down the hatches, keeping him busy weekends. He was content with his life in flux. He'd come to realize that movement was the norm, that the parts of a life are constantly in motion, even though it had seemed back then, back at the time that Missy had taken them on their naked adventure, that they were on a path toward permanence, that someday all the moving pieces of their lives would be locked down in place, a glossy, finished product of sorts. Bucky remained the philosopher, explaining to Jerry how the furniture he crafted was already in the tree, that he could see it there, and had only to free it. Jerry remembered his theory that night, over thirty years before, that there was no distinction in memory between the real, the remembered and the imagined. Now, Jerry believed it—or, as Bucky was fond of saying, *And oh, 'tis true, 'tis true.* Now, the memory of young men in garish gold uniforms on the deck that used to be, of naked bodies in the dark waters of the County Club pool, of a bug flying up Sally's nose, are entangled with the sock hop and Gloria's bleeding foot, with the sunny afternoon at the dam years before when a twelve-year-old boy broke his neck and died. The boy had yellow hair. And Jerry may or may not have actually been there to bear witness.

THE ESCAPEE'S LOVER

Seems like every time you turn around, they're carting somebody else out to die. Somebody takes a stroke or a heart attack, they carry them on up to the hospital to die, or over next door to the Memorial Home. As a general rule, they don't like anybody dying here. Me, I'm planning on getting out of here on my own two feet.

They call this place the Darius Litch *House*, not *Home*, which ought to give you a clue right there. It's over a hundred years old, and you could sail a kite in the drafts from the windows. They really knew how to waste space back in them days. There's new carpets laid down all over the place, nice and thick, so your hip won't bust so easy when you trip over your shoelace, and we got a piano up in the parlor and a TV in every room—regular lap of luxury. Even got a bunch of birds in cages and our own damn cat. I always been a dog man. For years I seen the place every day when I delivered beer across the street—used to have my own distributorship, but I wound up drinking more than what I sold. If you'd told me I was going to end up here myself, I'd of said you were crazier than all the old coots in it.

I'd only been in a few weeks when Missy busted me out. I'd already busted out a few times on my own, I don't recall how many. What I do recall is I was setting there planning my next one, setting down there at the end of the hallway, near the door. Of course they were on to me by then and had Elroy, the janitor, keeping an eye on me. Elroy's big as an outhouse, but not near as smart. One time they told him to feed the birds and let out the cat, but he fed the cat and let out the birds. Must not of fed the cat enough, though, cause then she ate two of the birds.

Ruthie wandered down the hall to where me and Elroy was setting staring one another down. All Ruthie ever does is sleep and wander, wander and sleep. She's the judge's widow. Missy's her kid, hers and the judge's. Ruthie's got yellow hair, and she don't look half bad if you squint your eyes to look at her. Ruthie says, "Aren't they going to feed us?"

I said, "It ain't suppertime yet."

That didn't make a dent. "They *have* to feed us sometime," she said.

"They just *fed* us."

She stood there with her chin up. Her hands was working. It was like she was knitting, but there wasn't any knitting needles in her hands. "We are supposed to have regular, nutritious meals. That is what we are paying for."

"They just fed us our lunch," I said. "We had hamburgs."

Ruthie looked down her nose at me. There's a haze in her eyes, like little clouds. "Those were not hamburgs," she says. "Those were meat patties."

You can't leave. If you just sashay on out the door, the alarm goes off, and they just come out and grab you in the parking lot—I ain't as quick as I used to be. There's this keypad contraption by the door and if you punch in the right numbers the alarm don't go off when you open it up. But nobody'll tell you what the right numbers are to punch in. I was setting there watching for somebody else to leave, figuring I could slip out then. But Elroy was setting there watching me watching.

Brenda the fat nurse comes wheeling her cart down the hall. "Chester," she says, "what are we doing?"

"I don't know about you," I said, "but I'm setting here minding my own business. You oughta give it a try sometime."

"Aren't we forgetting something?" I checked my fly—it was up. My shirt was buttoned, more or less, my shoes were tied, and I had at least two socks on. Brenda said, "We know we're not supposed to take our picture out of our room."

I clamped my arm down over it. "It's my *wife's* picture."

"We could fall and break the glass and cut ourselves."

"Or we could go peddle our pills someplace else."

"Do you want to give it to me, or do you want Elroy to take it?"

"Neither!"

Elroy grabbed the picture, and lifted me clean up out of the chair with it. That's when Missy comes in, just as we were tussling for it. Wasn't much of a tussle. Missy had her sunglasses on, and she smiled like she walked in on a tussle every day, like we were putting on a show just for her. Then she looks over top of her sunglasses at my picture Elroy had grabbed. "What a pretty girl," she says.

Brenda shakes her head and clucks her teeth, and says, "Chester, you better start behaving yourself if you want to stay here."

"I don't want to stay here!"

Brenda smiled. "Where you gonna go to?"

Ruthie was wandering around up at the other end of the hallway, where the couches are at. When she saw Missy she came down and went to give her kisses, but she missed. It put me in mind of a fish trying to breathe. Then Missy took Ruthie by the hand and led her back up the hallway toward her room, and Missy looked back over her shoulder at me. I didn't remember the last time a woman looked at me like that, and it took me back, way back, to some place I couldn't quite get to because it stopped just before I got there.

There was maybe twenty old women in the Darius Litch House, me and old Yeaney. Me and Yeaney as a matter of fact were the only two in the whole place that had balls. Why is it women live so much longer than men? I got my own theory. We spend all our lives pumping them full, they spend all theirs draining us dry. Simple as that. In the long run, it's bound to tell.

Old Yeaney must have been damn near a hundred. He just set up there all day long on the couch in the hallway with his cane poking up between his legs, his hands resting on top of it like it was his pecker. He hadn't said nothing all day long. Hell, I seen him go a week without saying nothing. You wouldn't know if he was alive or dead. Then all of a sudden he looks up and says, "Ice cream and cookies—that's what I need!"

Damned if Brenda doesn't go and get him some ice cream and cookies.

There's two of them little couches up in the hallway there—loveseats, they call them—right where the stairs come down and another hall heads up the other way. Everybody likes to set out there on the couches instead of in the parlor right around the corner where the piano and the birds are at. They're afraid they'll miss something if they ain't out there in the hallway. And if they're missing something, they figure they might as well already be dead.

Two old women, Hazel and Alverta, were setting on the couch next to Yeaney where they usually sat. Hazel was skinny and white, except for her eyes which was red and hard. Alverta was all fat and saggy, and her hair looked like worn-out porcupine quills.

Missy and Ruthie come walking up the hall. Hazel said, "Who are you?"

"Why that's Ruthie's daughter," Alverta said.

"No it ain't," Hazel said.

Missy just smiled. She still had her sunglasses on.

Just then Yeaney starts hacking up a storm. Yeaney had black lung. When he got to hacking good, he sounded like he was trying to cough one up. "Yeaney, please," Hazel said, "we got company." So Yeaney quit coughing. Then he leans over on one cheek and cuts one loose. Never even bats an eye.

"Why does he lean over on one buttock like that?" Ruthie said.

"So he don't shoot straight up in the air," Alverta said, and Hazel come out with a red-eyed cackle.

Ruthie said, "Is he eating ice cream and *cookies?*" She couldn't believe it.

Missy said, "Mother. I think *The Price is Right* is on."

"Wonderful," Ruthie said.

For a little while there, everything seemed to stand still. Missy and Ruthie up at the end of the hallway just out of one another's reach, Yeaney and the old women setting on their loveseats. Maybe the word *wonderful* was what done it. The sun was shining in on my cheek through the glass up over the door, and then I seen the cat asleep on the windowsill by the green plant. I smelled something that smelled like raw potatoes, and it put me in mind of my Helen fixing supper and how the knife used to click on the kitchen counter, and how the onions used to sizzle in the frying pan. That lasted maybe an hour, and then Missy comes walking down the hall toward me all by herself. She punched the number in, and opened the door. Then she stands there holding the door open, staring back at me over top of her sunglasses. "Well?" she says.

Elroy's chair was empty. I said, "Hold on a minute."

"Don't forget your picture," she said.

I said, "That's what I'm going for." Elroy was up on the stepladder changing a light bulb. He never even seen me. He was trying to figure out which way to twist the bulb.

Missy used to wreck cars. That's about the extent of my recollection of her. She used to hang around the bars when she first got to drinking age, but I hadn't seen her in years, till she come in one day to visit Ruthie. I remember one car, a green Mercury, she rolled it over so hard the jack was sticking straight up through the trunk lid like an arrow somebody shot through it. But she never killed nobody, and her old man was the judge, so nothing much ever come of it. Then she got married and moved off.

She said, "You're Chester Emerick, aren't you? Chet. I remember you. You used to deliver beer." Her voice was kind of deep, like an echo out of a well. She took off her sunglasses and cleaned them with the hem of her skirt, which was red. Her eyes was all puffy.

I said, "How come your folks named you Missy? Didn't they think you was ever going to grow up?"

"No, and they were right. Hop in." It was a little red car with bucket seats I wasn't sure I'd be able to climb out of. But I didn't have no place else to go. "This thing got safety belts?"

She laughed. "I'm all grown up now, Chet. I haven't wrecked a car in probably a week."

"How about I buy you a drink?"

"You sweet-talker." She nodded across the street toward the Pub Bar. "Over there?"

"They don't serve me over there. Last time they just called them up on the phone to come over and get me."

"How about the Green Lantern?"

"They don't serve me in there either."

"The Golden Bull?"

"Nope."

"You still barred from Jum's too?"

I just looked at her. I couldn't remember. I drew a blank on Jum's. She had a little grin. I wasn't sure there was any place in town that was going to serve me anymore. "I'm just teasing you, Chet," she said. "Jum's has been closed for years."

"I ain't got any money on me," I said.

"My treat. How about the Holiday Inn?"

It was out by the Interstate. "That sounds good. That oughta do just fine."

They wouldn't serve me there either. They had my picture taped up by the cash register next to a bunch of bounced checks. Missy said, "I know a place," and she took me for a ride.

She must've been going a hundred. I kept a hold of my picture. Kept it face down on my lap. We'd crest a hill and glide down and then up again, and from up on top you could see pastures and farms and woods, all laid out for miles around in the sun. I felt like I was flying. I felt like I could whip Elroy. Some noise was on the radio, and what with that and the wind in my ears, I didn't have to try to think any. I didn't know where I was, or where we were going to, but I'd been there before, so it felt like going home. Missy turned down the radio, reached over and tapped my picture. "Is that your little girl?"

"That's my old lady. Helen."

"You know, they have wallet-sized pictures. Pictures that fit in your wallet."

"I ain't got a wallet."

"So how come you lug it around like that?"

I lied. "Just to piss 'em off."

"You sure it isn't your little girl? She looks awful young."

"Well she ain't awful young. She's dead."

"Who? Your wife or your little girl?"

I had to think. "Yep."

"I'm sorry."

"You just get to where you're sick and tired of it all."

"Yes, you do," Missy said. We swooped down around a banked curve and swooped back out again, but my stomach kept heading out toward a big silo in the field. We come on this big old Buick doing about thirty, and Missy slammed on the brakes, honked her horn and zipped around it. There was an old woman driving it. She bowed her head at us like we were on a mission from the Government.

"So how's my mom doing?" Missy said. "Ruthie."

"Ruthie? She's a bubble or two off plumb."

"Do you think she's happy?"

"Hell no, I don't think she's happy. Happy?"

She smiled. I wasn't expecting that. "You reap what you sow, Chet. What goes around comes around—kind of like a boomerang, don't you think?"

My brain was beginning to itch. "If you say so."

"Sometimes I go into the Darius Litch House, and I don't even go to her room. Did you ever notice that? I go up and sit in the parlor all by myself, just to listen to the birds." She looked over at me, and I pointed toward the road. "And there's poor mommy just down the hallway waiting for me, wondering where in the world I could be."

I took my eyes off the road long enough to look at her.

"Oh, dear, what can the matter be?" Missy sang with a little grin, "oh, dear, what can the matter be?" I pointed toward the road.

She said she lived in Grayville. Or Grave Hill. I ain't sure which. She pulled up in the parking lot of some motor lodge place, and in we went. It was a lounge, not a bar. As a general rule, I don't like lounges, but the beer was cold, and you can't ruin a good shot of Seven. She started in on the Margaritas. The bartender was some kid in a yellow vest who kept looking at us like we just climbed out of a flying saucer. He was as good as invisible to Missy. She played some country tunes on the juke box, and told him to crank it up. She lit up a smoke and looked like she could of lived there, perched up on the barstool with her legs crossed and her skirt hiked up. Legs weren't half bad, either.

I couldn't get a fix on the room. There was walls of mirrors in front of other mirrors, and walls made out of glass bricks, and black walls with little spots of colored lights, and half walls, and walls every which way. All kinds of angles and steps and levels. One big wall of windows with red curtains that were glowing from the sun outside. I had to grab a hold of the bar to keep from sliding off.

I got hungry. They didn't have any pigs' knuckles or pickled eggs. Damned lounges. Kid give us a bowl of goldfish, little crackers. Turned my fingers yellow. Missy didn't eat any. She said she hardly ever ate, and she was skinny enough I believed her. The opposite of Ruthie, always worrying where her next meal's coming from.

So we drank to Ruthie. We drank to Missy's three husbands she told me she'd been through one at a time. We drank to Helen, and we drank to cancer. She didn't want to drink to the judge. She said, "Fuck the judge," then she giggled and said, "Pardon my French." She told me now that I'd got old, I reminded her of the judge. She called me the poor man's Herman Foulkrod. That was the judge's name. So we drank to poor men, then we drank to sons you ain't heard from in years, and to little girls who grow up into fat women and move down to Florida. She said she didn't have no kids to drink to. So we drank to grandsons who rob all your money, and stick you up in the Darius Litch House. She was doing shots and beers by now too. She kept buying, I kept drinking. I recall when I used to keep buying, to keep the women drinking. I figured she was out to get me drunk.

It worked. Willie Nelson come on singing a song I remembered was one I used to like, and so I told her I loved her.

"You sweet-talking son of a bitch," she said.

I said, "You're the only woman for me."

"Stop it Chester, or I'm gonna get naked right here."

"Me too."

She took a puff, and the end of her cigarette lit up. "How long's it been since you got laid, you old coot?"

I said, "What time is it now?"

I really did love her. It had crossed my mind that I might never get drunk again, and while I know good and well that drinking's the source of all my misery, I know even better it's my only source of comfort. Missy was my goddamn Florence Nightingale. There was little drops of sweat on her forehead. I never looked at her face before. There was a little drop of sweat in the corner of her eye. Her make-up was too thick and starting to crack, and her eyes were all black like the wall with the little colored lights.

"Let's dance," she said. "Here, Helen can't see us," and she put her picture face down on the bar. We danced some, but I don't move around so good anymore. Helen didn't miss nothing.

◆   ◆   ◆

I must've rested my eyes. I remember hearing voices in the dark. It was happy hour by then, and the noise was louder when your eyes were closed. I guess it's true blind people hear better than we do. I could hear every ice cube clink and every Zippo click and every ashtray sliding on the bar and every beer pop open and the gurgle of every pour. Somebody said, *Who are you?* and I heard Missy say, *I'm daddy's little girl,* and there was laughing and chattering and people all talking at the same time. Somebody said, *What do you do?* and Missy said, *Margaritas mostly, a CC-water-back now and then, and every so often a shot of Jim Beam. You name it.* Then I heard more. I heard plenty. I heard Yeaney hacking up a storm and the old hens clucking and the alarm whining at the Darius Litch House and Helen crying and my old man saying the Lord's Prayer. I heard Missy laughing like a crazy woman on top of the pool table in Jum's that's been closed now for years. Pool balls clacking and glass breaking. I heard the bell bonging twelve o'clock from the Court House tower and I heard the police siren and the crack of my granddaddy's rifle and a deer tumbling through the brush. I heard rain falling on the tin roof of the shed right outside my bedroom window after Helen wasn't there to hear it no more. I heard the wind blowing and the sun shining. Then I heard the kid in the yellow vest saying, *I think you and your father have had enough,* and I heard Missy call him a snot-nosed little shit.

She was pulling me up out of the car in some strange place. It was a field of some kind. The air cleaned out my head, right through my nose and out my ears. There was a few trees throwing long shadows across the way. And there was fog, little puddles of it laying down on the ground. I said, "Ain't this fog upside down?" I couldn't find my feet.

Missy said, "You must have to pee. You haven't peed in a long time."

I started crying. I couldn't help it. Nobody ever cared if I peed before. I said, "I do."

"Over this way," Missy said.

I stepped on something hard. "What's this?"

"That's one of the markers. They have them flat so they can mow."

I kicked the fog away. It said *George Allshouse 1916 – 1981.* "We in Grave Hill?"

"No. This is the cemetery."

Across a little rise I made out a statue of two big hands holding a book open. Must've been the Bible, I figured. They were tucked in a nest of spruce trees. Biggest hands I ever seen. Down the other way I made out a mound of rocks with golden letters on it that said *Babyland.* "Says over there we're in Babyland."

"That's the part of the cemetery where they bury babies," she said. "They bury babies for free, in hopes their parents'll buy a plot then."

"That's a pretty good deal," I said.

"Are you crying, Chet?"

"No, I ain't crying."

"You are too. How come?"

I lied. "All them dead babies."

"You'll feel better after you pee," she said, and I started crying even more.

Missy hiked her skirt up, tugged her underpants down— they was red too—and squatted down to pee. "Why, you're pissing on somebody's grave, ain't you?" I said, wiping my eyes. I listened to the splash.

She didn't say anything right away. She really had to pee. She must've been saving it up. Finally she let out a little sigh and said, "The judge's. I bring all my boyfriends here to pee."

I walked over for a look. Sure enough: *The Honorable Herman Morris Foulkrod 1900 – 1975.* If I'd of been thinking, I'd of wondered why Missy would want to go and piss on her old man's grave, but I wasn't. He was sheriff before he was judge, and he'd threw me in jail a couple times, so I kind of took to the idea of pissing on his grave.

"How about your husbands?"

"Them too. In fact I brought my whole group out here one time to pee on his grave."

"A whole group?" I said. She'd stood up again by now. "All at the same time?"

"Yeah. It was kind of crazy." She looked down to admire her little puddle in the fog. "Well hurry up."

"I can't with you watching me."

"I'll walk over here," she said.

"I got one of them bashful bladders."

"I'll take a stroll through Babyland."

I listened to her strolling away, whistling "She'll Be Coming 'Round the Mountain." The fog was up to my knees. I was sinking in it. I closed my eyes to concentrate, and started swaying. I really wanted to piss on the judge's grave in the worst way and make Missy proud of me. I thought about heavy rain and tinkling brooks and raging rivers, and imagined Niagara Falls beating down all around my head. I imagined the fog coming up all around me, and those big stone hands lifting me up like a dandelion out of the yard, and big stone lips blowing me away like fluff flying out across the twilight.

"I love you, Sweetie." It was Missy. Woke me up. We were in her car, and it was dark outside. I said, "I love you too, Sweetie."

Missy said, "I miss you so much." She was crying.

Then I seen she wasn't talking to me. She was turned away from where I was setting, toward the window on the driver's side. Then I seen she had one of them mobile telephone contraptions. It was foggy outside. There was this row of bright lights in the dark, big glowing balls going smaller out away into nothing.

She quit talking, and I said, "Who was that?"

Missy sniffed, and wiped at her cheek. "That was my little girl. Katie."

"Thought you said you didn't have no kids."

"I lied. Katie lives with her father in Virginia. God only knows what he's doing to her."

She didn't say nothing else. I said, "Where we at?"

"I have to go back to Grayville." Or Grave Hill.

"My legs is kinda chilly."

"You took your pants off."

I couldn't remember taking them off, but I figured I must've had a good reason, so I didn't say nothing. The row of lights wasn't throwing any our way, and I couldn't see much. She was beside me like a shadow. She wiped her eyes again, and pressed at her cheeks like she was putting on a new face. The fog was white around the lights, and I was wondering how far away they went when I seen a red one floating in toward us, and I heard this roar commencing that got so loud I could feel it in my chest. And I was just about to figure out that we were at the county airport when Missy reached over and cupped her hand around my privates. It was like she put them in an oven. I started feeling toasty all over.

She whispered in my ear. "Does that feel good, Chet? Do you like that?" Her voice was way down at the bottom of the well. Like someplace where it shouldn't have been.

"Don't feel too bad," I said.

"Did you make your little girl do this?"

I didn't know what she meant.

"Did you?" She started squeezing.

"Can I have my pants back now?"

"Did you have your pants on when you slipped down the hallway, Chet?" She squeezed harder. "While Helen was sleeping? Or pretending to?"

"What hallway's that?"

She gave a real hard squeeze that bounced me up on my best behavior. "The hallway to your little girl's room, Chet. That hallway."

They say your life passes before your eyes. A little bit of mine did. Quite a bit, I guess, considering the big chunks of it that are already AWOL. There was a lot of backseats and alleys and cheap motels and women that wasn't my Helen. There was a big cloud of smoke and the smell of booze, and foggy barroom lights, and my ma standing next to the old man's grave trying to hide her cigarette behind her dress. I was scared. I didn't know what to say. It just came out. "I ain't the poor man's Herman Foulkrod," I said.

She turned loose of my privates. She started crying again. She buried her face in my shirt, and just set there sobbing. "I know," she said. "He's dead. The son of a bitch."

We sat there for a little while. Missy was shivering. She was just a little girl.

I put my arms around her, kept her warm. I said, "This here's been the best day of my life."

I watched the lights of the planes roaring in and out, and figured Missy was on one of them. After a while, I seen a little light come bouncing out toward me through the fog. This guy with an Avis hat come out to check for gas and mileage, and see if there was any dents or scratches on his car. Must've knew how Missy drove. When he seen me, he jumped back, startled. He shined his light in on me. "What are you doing in there?"

I shrugged. "Just setting."

"Where the hell's your pants?"

I just shrugged again.

Old Yeaney up and died about a month later. They'd let me back in the Darius Litch House, and I'd been figuring I wasn't going to be busting out again. Least that's what I figured at first. But by the time old Yeaney died, my mind was starting to waffle on it. Matter of fact, I was setting back down there at the end of the hallway, watching the door.

Missy hadn't been back to visit Ruthie since the day she busted me out and left me without any pants. Took some time till that sank all the way into my brain. Figured for a while there she must've just been drunk or crazy or both. But then I was setting there in the corner with the cat on my lap one day, watching Hazel and Alverta squabbling over their Scrabble game, when it come to me like one of them light bulbs going off over your head in a cartoon. It was clear as a bell to me what had happened. I seen him there, the judge, naked and sweaty underneath his long, black robe, slinking down a long, black hallway, slinking straight down towards hell.

Ruthie come wandering toward me. Now I knew why she spent her days wandering down hallways. She didn't say nothing to me, just looked at me and sniffed like she could smell something bad, then turned around and moseyed on up past Hazel and Alverta. She set down next to Yeaney on the other loveseat. Yeaney was already dead, but nobody knew it. He set there dead for the better part of the day, and nobody knew it.

Ruthie started talking to him. Everybody was used to him setting there asleep, so nobody give it much thought. He was setting there like he always was, with his hands on his cane. Ruthie asked him when they were going to feed us, but of course Yeaney, being dead, didn't have much to say.

Alverta said, "Somebody stinks." Hazel scrunched her red eyes up, and sniffed.

Ruthie looked at them, and Alverta said, "Better not sit there, Ruthie. I think Yeaney pooped his pants again."

Hazel says, "Abandon ship!"

Brenda the fat nurse come out of a room across the hall and says, "Yeaney, did you have another accident? Yeaney?"

She reached down and shook his shoulder to wake him up, and knew right away he was dead. She says, "Oh no," and called the head nurse who called the supervisor, and pretty soon the whole hallway filled up. A couple nurses from over at the Memorial Home come running in and scared the cat, who raced off. The birds up in the parlor started squawking and carrying on. Ruthie couldn't figure out what all the fuss was about, why everybody was standing around gawking at her and Yeaney.

Brenda said, "Ruthie, get up. Get up, Ruthie. Yeaney's passed on."

Ruthie was in a snit cause she had to get up. She didn't like all the commotion. She wandered toward me, back at the end of the crowd. I was the only man in the place now, at least the only one still breathing.

Ruthie says, "Does this mean they're not going to feed us?"

I said, "Yep. Sure looks that way."

She looks at me like somebody just tore her heart out.

I said, "Tell you what, Ruthie old girl. I'll go out and pick us a mess of sprouts and greens and you can fry 'em up in your frying pan." She didn't like that idea. She looked down her nose at me, from behind them little clouds in her eyes.

TICKLE ME GEORGE

George Northey believed there was something to the old clichés about the jolly fat man, the sad fat man, the sensitive fat man. Simply by virtue of his size, there was more of him to absorb the emotion, more volume within which it could roll around, snowball, gather momentum from heart to brain. So his reaction when he spotted his wife, Cathy, across the crowded mall was not surprising: Beyond excitement—joy! Here he was, fifty miles from home, completely unaware that she was showing a house in the area. What were the odds? Was this his day, or what?

"Is that your mommy?" he said to his two-and-a-half-year-old daughter.

"Mommy?" Ellen strained forward.

George loved it when she understood, when his words hit their mark. "I think so. She went into that Bugaboo Creek Steakhouse place."

"Bugaboooo?" Ellen said perfectly.

He hurried toward the restaurant with a feeling of

omniscience, about to bring shock and delight into the day of his wife. Although hurrying was problematic; after two hours Christmas shopping in the mall, sweat stains drooped from his armpits like maps of Africa. The gifts he'd found so far were cumbersome and heavy, particularly the wrought iron floor lamp, boxed and bulky, which had replaced Ellen in the stroller. His daughter rode in one arm, more boxes and bags in the other. She was sweating too, wispy blond hair clinging to her neck. She put her hand on the clammy front of her father's shirt, her face frowning earnestly, and said with a concerned squeal, "Het, daee?"

Wet or sweat? Whichever; with the bulk of his three hundred pounds between his shoulders and hips—a heart attack waiting to happen, or so he'd heard a hundred times— he understood her concern. "Just a little damp, honey." He'd heard it through the grapevine that Kaybee Toys in the Mulberry Mall had Tickle Me Elmo dolls—this year's Christmas treasure—well worth the trek from Hartsgrove if true. He shared with Elmo a penchant for the nervous giggle, and felt the doll would make a nice memento to remind Ellen of her daddy if what was waiting to happen ever did. The grapevine, though, had been wrong.

Nevertheless, he'd stayed to shop. There were no malls at all in Hartsgrove, and the nearest, the Harmony Mall, was much smaller than the Mulberry. He'd wrested the Christmas shopping chores away from his wife, Cathy, citing his more abundant free time, though the real reason was her more expensive tastes. She did well enough at the real estate agency, but his antiques business was dormant, if not dead, and his part-time job at the supermarket paid little. Cathy, raised well-off, disdained budgets, but George, raised not so well-off, was the realist. Also, he liked Christmas shopping. Though this he'd never admit to his friend, Strauss the butcher.

At the entrance to the Bugaboo Creek Steakhouse, he hesitated. What was wrong with this picture? Itching with anticipation, he didn't take time to decipher it. He didn't pause long enough to think how unlike his wife it was to dine in such a place alone, though that might have been the very thought—unborn—that caused his hesitation, that caused him to stop just inside the restaurant doorway beneath a talking moose head, holding Ellen behind a plastic boulder where she couldn't see. Where he quickly spotted Cathy. George stood round and hollow, inflated by the big, fat emotion careening within him, buffeting his heart and brain. At first, he couldn't be sure the woman was her. Her features were distorted, nearly unrecognizably, by the intense happiness blazing on her face as she sat holding the hand of a man he had never seen before.

George retreated with haste and stealth, as much haste and stealth as a screaming toddler and a mountain of packages and fat would allow, even as he was quite unaware of the retreat. He was through the parking lot and to his car before awareness began to return. Everything beyond the confines of his brain had diminished to white noise as his mind went about its business of wonder, shock and recovery. Even Ellen's insistent iteration, "Daee foo my tor heat!" he never bothered to attempt to translate, talking to her instead, as he always did, a warm, reassuring, steady stream of words he never heard himself. He felt faint, slightly wobbly. Something had irrevocably shifted beneath his feet, and he no longer stood on the same solid ground as before.

He'd settled into the drive, the Pennsylvania countryside melding into a dirty snow blur of barns and farms, fields and fences, when he began doubting his own eyes. Maybe it had been another woman, a woman who resembled Cathy; the place had been packed, the room dim. He had nearly convinced himself she was wearing a green sweater, not the blue one Cathy had on this morning, when he remembered what he'd read about near-death experiences: that the bright, loving light, the euphoria were only the mind's way of trying to ease the pain of death. Surely such a kind mind would change the color of a sweater in a wink.

Then he remembered Cathy telling him her brother was coming to visit—a surge of relief. Her brother lived in Florida, and George hadn't seen him in nine years. He dredged his mind for details but came up empty. He was cruising. Around a bend, he came to a long, flat straightaway, three silos of a large dairy farm framed by the hills at the far end of the stretch. Before he reached the silos, his sense of relief had withered and blown away. Why would Cathy meet her brother for lunch 50 miles from home?

Raymond was next. From nowhere, the name bubbled to the surface. George could not remember how or why he knew the name; it was just there. He adjusted his mirror to see Ellen in the back, strapped and napping in her car seat. Her lips moved, a series of nonsense sounds sneaking out of her sleep. Cathy talked in her sleep too. She often woke him. He was a light sleeper, getting lighter, and it suddenly burst upon him like the sweat bursting across his brow, that sleep was the source of *Raymond*. Had he heard Cathy mention him in her sleep? Or was Raymond his own private nightmare? This much he knew: *Raymond knows how to treat a lady.* George didn't slow for the next sweeping curve; braking was not in the script. Gripping the wheel with his white, fat fists, he let gravity and centrifugal force have at it, letting them have their way with him. He was only along for the ride.

Cathy came home only a little late, alone. Her face was flushed, accentuating the flaws of her complexion. She had been rushing, she explained, stopping to pick up noodles for lasagna, George's favorite. Only it wasn't George's favorite. It was also incompatible with the Dr. Atkins Diet, which she knew he'd been on these past two months or more. He was never particularly fond of lasagna in the first place, and exactly how Cathy had come to believe it was his favorite was lost in history, but he'd always let the misunderstanding stand rather than hurt her feelings.

He made the salad. "How's your brother?" he asked, slicing a cucumber on the nineteenth-century butcher block.

Cathy, laying noodles, paused. "He's fine. I told you I talked to him last week, didn't I?"

"Yes. When's he coming up?"

"June. Weren't you listening?"

"I guess I missed some of it." He frowned at the salad bowl. "That was the night Ellen went potty."

Ellen, scribbling with a crayon in a real estate brochure, looked up from the kitchen floor. "Poddy?"

"And I was so proud of you!" Cathy said. Ellen with a delighted squeal came running to be swept up in mommy's arms. "Such a big girl!" Cathy said.

"Bugaboo!" said Ellen.

"What honey?"

"Bugabooooo!" said Ellen, shouting the last happy syllable at the ceiling.

Cathy turned to George. "What's she saying?"

"Sounds like Bugaboo," said George, eyebrows arching. His was a wide open face that couldn't hide whatever the emotion behind it; his eyebrows defied gravity, arching whenever he began to speak, or listen, or anything in between, an unmasking, an involuntary emphasis to his sincerity, enhanced by the baldness of his head, the broadness of his smile and the brown warmth of his eyes. Though now the smile was faltering.

Cathy put her daughter down; Ellen raced off. George put his knife down, watching his wife. She was small, a foot shorter than him and as she looked up, confusion clutched her face; it was pinched and narrow, the skin less than smooth and he could understand why some might think her homely; but to him she was beautiful, vulnerable as a baby. Her icy eyes had always seemed a plea to George, a plea for a big, warm hug. As she wiped her hands on her apron, he could see that the time had come to talk. He could see it in her face. Confession, deception, explanation, whatever; the time had come. It made him shiver, not only the brink of revelation, but at how they'd already communicated, wordlessly, soul to soul.

"Do you want meatballs in this?" Cathy said.

George took his coffee break with his friend Strauss the butcher, sitting among prime cuts and bloodstains in the back of the Golden Days Supermarket. When George struggled to open his big bag of pork rinds with the bright red *Paid* tag on it, gnawing at the top with his teeth, Strauss took the bag and slit it end to end with a large knife, helping himself to a handful. Strauss was skinny, wiry as a greyhound.

"All set for Christmas, Don?" George asked.

The voice of Mrs. Leech from the office crackled unintelligibly over the speaker before Strauss could reply.

"I guess, George. I pretty much let the old lady take care of that."

"Me too." George gulped at his sugarless coffee. "Speaking of the old lady, a funny thing happened to a friend of mine," he said. "I know what you're thinking, the old 'friend of mine' bull, but this really *is* a friend of mine. That's the trouble when something happens to a friend, it's always hard to tell somebody about it cause they never really believe it's a friend and not you." Strauss assured

George he believed him. George told Strauss how his friend thought he saw his wife having lunch with a strange man, holding his hand and happy. Very happy. His friend wasn't sure what to do. Trouble was, his friend still wasn't convinced he saw what he might have seen.

"George, I guess if I was you I'd tell my friend that first of all he has to decide that he saw what he saw. Then he has to find out who he saw and why, you know, make sure it wasn't something legit, just a misunderstanding or something. Then when that's all over and done with, he takes a knife like this here one and cuts the guy's balls off."

George giggled nervously. His friend Strauss spent too much time smelling raw meat. "This friend of mine, he's really not the violent type."

"Yeah, yeah. Nobody's the violent type till somebody's dicking his wife."

The voice of Mrs. Leech repeated the garbled message on the speaker. George said, "And I've never really understood that anyway. Wouldn't it be more *her* fault than his?"

"Maybe, George, but you can't cut *her* balls off."

Not wanting to hurt Strauss's feelings, George felt as though he should giggle again, but couldn't bring himself to. "Actually, my friend's more the forgiving kind."

"Who is it?" Strauss asked.

"My friend?"

"Yeah."

"This guy I know from out of town."

"Tell your friend if he wants I know somebody that can find out exactly what's going on for him," Strauss said. "Buddy of mine, Benny Garvey, he used to be a cop over in Roseport, he does a little private dick work on the side. He's cheap. If you say you know me."

"I don't think he'd go for anything like that." George wondered how much was cheap.

"Well just to let you know. To let *him* know."

Mrs. Leech popped through the swinging doors with evident irritation. "Clean-up in aisle three, George," she said. "Didn't you hear me? Somebody busted a big jar of applesauce."

After work, George brought the daily bag of groceries into his mother's small apartment. With a lunge, push and wobble, she rose from the old recliner for her daily hug. A news show on the television was so low he was certain she couldn't hear a word of it. She was hard of hearing. So when he stayed to chat, as he did every day, he chatted loudly, knowing that despite her smiles and nods of interest, she missed a great deal of what he said. His mother loved to talk even more than he did, and since his father had died five years ago, she seldom had the opportunity, though she confided in George that talking to his father had often been like talking to an empty room. She told George again that Mrs. McManigle had died. And again that Emory Chestnut had cancer. She had written a letter to her landlord stating her case for new carpeting—this he heard for the first time. But she quickly compensated by telling him for the third time how Mrs. Harriger was getting crazier and crazier, how she had recently put the phone down to make her lunch while Mrs. Harriger had rattled on and on. In turn, he told her every cute Ellen anecdote he could muster (he might repeat himself too, albeit intentionally, if the anecdote was over a week old), and filled her in on his and Cathy's jobs, reminding her again that the antique shop was closed for the winter. If not for good, he didn't add. At 74, his mother had worries enough.

For the same reason, he was careful to maintain his normal demeanor, to not allow a hint of his anxiety to creep to the surface of his chatter, particularly when he spoke of

Cathy or Ellen. George didn't want to burden his mother; there was nothing she'd love more, he knew, than a fresh opportunity to worry over him.

"I just heard on the radio there's going to be a full moon on Christmas Eve. First time since 1950." Whenever he could, he liked to take his mother back to the good old days. "I wasn't even a gleam in Dad's eye yet."

"No," his mother said. "You certainly wouldn't have been."

She said nothing for a while, which George found odd, but he could see the wheels turning behind her cloudy brown eyes. She made her way with difficulty across the thin carpet to part the blinds and peer outside toward the sky that would hold such a moon. George joined her by the window, and they watched the dusk slowly hiding the hills of Hartsgrove like a memory fading.

"That was the Christmas your father was gone," she said.

"I didn't know he was gone any Christmas."

"Yes. That was the year he was—" She hesitated, a sour look overcoming her face. "Down south looking for work. I didn't hear much from him. I didn't hear much from him at all."

"That was just after you were married, wasn't it?"

"Let's see. Yes. It was the second Christmas we were married."

Hartsgrove was his father's home town, not his mother's. "Did you have any friends? Did you know anybody here?"

"As a matter of fact, I did." To George's surprise, she said nothing else, and he again found the lull unusual. He quickly filled it, chatting till she was back on track; they chatted till he sensed she'd had her fill for this visit. Then he kissed her goodbye, left her in her recliner, and turned to leave. Once again, she surprised him, following him to the doorway.

"George," she said, her wispy gray eyebrows floating in concern, "is everything all right between you and Cathy?"

When he arrived home with Ellen from the sitter's, the red light on the phone was blinking. He pressed *Play*. Cathy's artificial voice said she would be late, she had to show the old Minick house again. Could he get himself and Ellen something to eat?

"Mommy!" said Ellen, pointing at the phone.

"That's your mommy."

"Mommy sic to ray man."

"What honey?" George said.

Ellen repeated herself, with great earnestness.

"Raymond? Did you say Raymond, honey?"

"Mommy sic to!"

"Raymond? Raymond who, honey? Who's Raymond?"

"Inna tor, daee," said Ellen, holding concerned fingers to her daddy's chin. George kissed her fingertip, reassuring her.

He prepared hot dogs for supper, quickly boiling six— Ellen, he knew, was good for at least a half—which they ate without bread, Ellen because that was her preference and George because that was Dr. Atkins's preference. "Shall we go for a ride and see the pretty Christmas lights, honey?"

"Go bye-byes? Piddy ites?"

Through the darkened streets of Hartsgrove, George pointed out each glittering display, the gaily lit trees, the candles in the windows, the random rooftop Santas. Ellen was impatient: "Piddy ites again," she demanded as soon as they had passed one if another was not immediately in sight. He lectured her on the virtues of patience. George talked to her constantly, little reassurances (how pretty she was and how smart), little lessons (the importance of patience, the real meaning of Christmas). This was how he communicated with her, subliminally. He knew she could understand little or none of what he told her, but hoped the words were absorbed in her mind, stored there for future use, when they could be released, drop by drop, time release capsules, palliatives for a lifetime of aches and pains. They bumped down the bricks of Pershing Street to Main Street wide and smooth, where the flood-lit, life-sized Nativity Scene highlighted the Courthouse Lawn, then up East Main and out Ruggles Road to the famous Chestnut display, dazzling and huge. Ellen oohed in proper appreciation as George revisited it several times, until finally he saw the yawns he'd been awaiting, saw the little head drooping.

There were no Christmas lights at the old Minick house. Ellen was sound asleep, head overflowing her shoulder. Behind the Sandy Lick Realty *For Sale* sign, the house sat back on a deep lot on the side of Rose Hill, one of Hartsgrove's steepest, and George turned his tires toward the curb when he parked. There were no lights at all and the undisturbed inch of snow on the drive and all around the house quickly told him that no one had been there tonight.

He looked at his sleeping daughter, her lips silently moving, mouthing the language of angels. Last night, Cathy had talked in her sleep again. Thinking he'd heard *Raymond*, he'd surfaced from somewhere between a daydream and a nightmare to wide-awake clarity. He'd listened intensely to each muted vibration of the air, each sigh and smack of lip, each syllable whispered and lost. He'd studied her sleeping cheek in the dim red glow of the digital numbers from her nightstand, 3:36 a.m. He'd heard a faint nasal click, then a pair: *na. Nad. Nod. Not. Not what* broke free from her dream, and George remembered the first words she'd ever spoken to him, red glow and all: "That's not what I meant."

She'd been shopping with her mother (their custom even still) the first time he saw her, at Northey's Antiques, a converted filling station on Main Street, after George's father had finally given up the ghost of interest, and had withdrawn with his ennui and his damaged back to the private hospice of his mind. Mrs. Reitz had been in the market for a chair to complement the decor—early *nouveau riche*, as George later discovered—of her new sitting room. George had showed them a lolling chair from the federal period and a mahogany fiddleback rocker, demonstrating the comfort of the latter. "I don't know," Mrs. Reitz had said. "It looks awfully fragile." "My God, mother," Cathy had said, "it holds *him*, doesn't it?" Then, face going scarlet, to George: "That's not what I meant."

He'd fallen in love with the scarlet, accentuating as it did the imperfections in her complexion like a fine, mellow patina. And he didn't mind the insult (he was after all a heart attack waiting to happen), for if anything, her embarrassment had helped cement the sale, and George had the name and address. And the excuse—the delivery—to see her again.

Ellen cried out from her car seat, and George held his breath for the sequel but only silence followed; it was just a bad dream. Just a bad dream. Through the snarl of naked tree limbs, he watched lights flicker on the far hillside and the steeple of the Catholic Church below him on the top of another hill, as he waited for the visitor he knew was never coming. He had always loved the hills of Hartsgrove but found his foot on the brake, pressing hard against the new, gnawing apprehension, this fear of falling.

They were fast dancing, not touching, till Cathy danced close enough to put her hand on the clammy front of George's shirt, and say with a mock frown, "Eeewe." It was their timeless charade; he knew she loved it. He knew it was his dancing, his sweating, his energy—his big fat *joie de vivre*—along with his gift of nervous gab, that persuaded her to fall in love with him those years ago. So on George danced, smile broad, eyebrows high and round, but this time she didn't dance her way into his arms for the next slow song; this time she danced away.

The Sandy Lick Realty Christmas party was at the home of the company's president, whom George saw but once a year, at the Christmas party. The food was good, the music loud, the Christmas lights flashy and the place packed with reveling realtors and their guests. George liked the party (he liked any party), one of the few Christmas parties where no one had ever asked him to play Santa.

Cathy danced away to mingle, pursue company politics. George taught the wife of the company president the electric slide, all the while watching from the corner of his eye his wife at her mingling. Her face was flushed and beautiful from the heat of the party, and as she threw back her head to laugh, cocking her wrist below the snugness of her sweater, he felt she had never looked more desirable. Sex with Cathy had been sadly infrequent the last three years, since the conception of Ellen.

She had been conceived after a party, a Halloween party. Had he had his way, it would have been years earlier, but he hadn't been able to overcome Cathy's misgivings about her lack of maternal instincts; he'd tried to persuade her that his own abundance would more than compensate, but to no avail.

After the Halloween party, a night of heavy dancing and sweating, he'd felt a crushing pain in his chest. The pain grew as the color drained, and the sweat flowed till his bald head glistened, and Cathy was convinced of the worst. She helped him to the car and raced to the Emergency Room of Hartsgrove Hospital where indigestion was finally diagnosed. Back home, she was as pale and drained as he. She seduced him—sans diaphragm—on the thick carpet by the curly maple Queen Anne settee in the den. "Damn it, George, don't you *ever* do that again," she'd whispered, "don't you *ever* try to leave me! You scared the *shit* out of me! You come right now!"

Cathy was passing among minglers when she paused alone beneath a sprig of mistletoe for only an instant. Through the swarming celebration, she was unaware that George was watching. He was watching the kiss she mouthed and the quick, loving glance she cast secretly from beneath the mistletoe toward someone across the room. Who? Was there a *Raymond* in the house? By the time George tracked her glance through the crowd, whoever had broken his big, fat heart had turned away from his swimming eyes.

Christmas Eve shoppers scattered before him like ducks before a boat as George steamed sweating down the wide aisle of the Golden Days Supermarket in response to Mrs. Leech's urgent crackle over the speaker. Beneath his arm was the large brown envelope Strauss the butcher had just thrust upon him, and George felt that everyone was staring at it, as they might at an ugly tumor. He wondered where he could safely stash it while he performed whatever emergency chore Mrs. Leech was crackling him unto.

"I talked to Garvey," Strauss had explained, handing him the envelope. "He followed your friend's wife around for a couple of days in his spare time."

Unsure if he should, George had glanced in the envelope at arm's length. He'd glimpsed a photo of Cathy smiling and walking into a house with a man, neither of which, house or man, he knew. A Sandy Lick Realty *For*

Sale sign was clearly visible. There were other photographs and at least two pages of typewritten text. George hadn't known what to say. "How much do I owe you?" he'd finally asked.

"This one's a freebee. Garvey owed me."

"Thanks. I guess I have to—I should probably—did you—"

"It's none of my business, George." In his hand, Strauss had gripped a meat cleaver impatiently, knuckles white, eyes smoldering in an odd mixture of shame and anger, before looking away. "Hey. I got problems of my own."

George had hidden behind his nervous giggle until Mrs. Leech had saved him.

Mrs. Leech looked up from behind the glass. "Yes?"

"I couldn't make out what you said."

"Oh I wasn't calling you, George. But while you're here, you can bag Wilda."

George bagged Wilda. Wilda Wingard was a nervous old lady of skin and bone, eyeballs magnified behind the thick lenses of her glasses. It was bad enough, what was in the envelope, but what was in Strauss's eyes was worse. Perhaps the cliché of violence—the cutting off of balls, the beating the shit out of—was mere hyperbole, but nevertheless, the essence remained: What sort of a man would not confront his wayward wife and her lover? Would simply slither out of the restaurant where they sat holding hands? What sort of a man would not seek—if not vengeance, at least justice, some small measure of retribution? The wobbly feeling was back, the ground still shifting beneath him, as he watched a drop of sweat fall from his face and splatter on Wilda's tomato.

George looked up. In his hand was a mangled loaf of bread. Several feet away, Wilda Wingard stood flinching and cringing.

◆   ◆   ◆

Later that afternoon, his mother told him a story that had obviously been on her mind. Sometimes things snagged there and clung for days. "One day we got a package in the mail from your father's Aunt Edith. I told him about it when he came home for lunch that day—he was working for Phil Bish then, that was before he started his own antiques. It wasn't too long after he came back home from Dayton. I remember we had roast beef sandwiches. He always ate two but of course I didn't make them near as thick then as they do nowadays. It was on a Monday, and he didn't say anything at all about it. Three days later, on Thursday, he came home for lunch and asked me what was in that package."

George wondered at the look on his mother's face, as though she had bitten a lemon. "What was in it?"

"Oh, I don't remember," she said with a dismissive wave, "it was so long ago."

George shrugged. "That was dad."

Across the room, Ellen looked up from the small ceramic Christmas tree on the coffee table before the wide window. "Daee?"

"*My* daddy," George explained. "Did you tell grandma Merry Christmas yet?"

"May kismas, gamma."

"Don't touch the tree, honey, just look at it," he said. "Aren't the lights pretty?"

Ellen said something else to her grandmother, something of great significance, judging by the look on her face. "What did she say, George?"

"Beats me. Something about Santa maybe?"

"Oh how exciting!" she said to Ellen. "Have you been a good girl?"

Ellen was not interested in that question. She picked up the miniature sleigh and reindeer, moving them from the coffee table to the window sill above. "What's going on with Cathy?" his mother asked.

George didn't say he'd told her already where Cathy was, fifteen minutes ago when they'd first arrived. "She had to go over to her mother's to help get ready for tomorrow. They have the whole family over."

"I know *that*, George. You told me that already."

"Piddy moooon," cooed Ellen, pointing through the window.

They crossed the room to see. A perfectly round white disk was low in the sky over the woods of Rose Hill. "Santa won't have any trouble finding our house tonight," George said.

"He won't need Rudolph," his mother said.

George and his mother both lingered, looking at the moon. Ellen was touching the tiny lights on the little ceramic tree. "First Christmas Eve full moon since 1950," George said. "Do you remember what you were doing 46 years ago tonight?"

"Yes," his mother said, "I do." She made her way back, to her chair, to her youth. "That was the year we went to see Harold Fyock's Christmas Display—do you remember that? A whole little village he built with all the trains running through it. It had streets and cars and hills and trees and lakes—no. I don't believe he still had it by the time you were old enough to remember. He kept adding to it, and it became quite famous. I think he moved it down to Pittsburgh."

"Who?"

"Why, Harold Fyock."

"No, who did you go see it with? That was the year dad was gone, and you said 'we.'"

"A friend of mine." For a moment his mother frowned, looked cross. "A very dear friend. He was a nurse up at the hospital with me. They didn't have many male nurses back in those days. He'd been a medic in the army during the war. Actually, he'd left town by then, but he came back to visit one last time."

"What was his name?"

"His name was Raymond. Raymond Shannon."

Blinking, George sat on the threadbare little sofa he'd been nearest. From her recliner, his mother cocked her head. "George? Are you all right?"

His first reaction had been astonishment at the coincidence—what were the odds?—but as the absorption of the name *Raymond* continued, it squeezed out the likelihood of chance. At the same time, he understood at a very basic, instinctual level, that he would never spend a minute mining for possible causes and meanings. He would only hope that he lived long enough for those causes and meanings to seek him out and reveal themselves.

His heart felt tight and heavy. And George realized that what he felt was the threat that had invaded his happy life, this menace that could seek him out, find him anywhere, even in the sanctuary of these quiet rooms where his mother chattered, where his little girl climbed atop his ample lap singing the simple verse to a happy song, without a single, recognizable word. And now he understood too that Raymond was not the threat. His wife's lover, whoever he was, was not the threat at all. It was him. The threat was the person that he was, himself, the weakling lurking in Strauss's eyes, the big, fat, bald, 40-year-old stock boy at the Golden Days Supermarket.

Returning the pliers and screwdriver to the toolbox in the cellar way, George waited. He was ready now, his fortress constructed, his loins girded. Upstairs in her bed, Ellen talked in her sleep, something garbled, a warning, totally unintelligible. He turned out the lamps on either side of the sofa, and adjusted a string of multi-colored lights on a low branch of the tree, raising it a limb, standing back to see how it would look when Ellen first saw it in the morning. Two logs burned meekly on a bed of coals in the fireplace. By the tree, her tricycle sat, a stuffed Barney doll grinning from the basket. He didn't regret failing to get the Tickle Me Elmo. George had decided that their common bond, his penchant for the nervous giggle, was a thing of the past.

He'd rushed to finish on time, before Cathy got home, and he'd made it. He was sweating, his heart racing, and it felt good. He paced, living room to dining room to kitchen, back around again, perpetuating the rush, enjoying the edge. Each pass through the dining room he stopped to look out the window at the empty driveway, his hand resting on the butternut tea table beside the brown envelope that Strauss had forced upon him.

At last he heard Cathy's car in the drive. It was nearly midnight, nearly Christmas morning. He stood watching through the window in the dining room, at the edge of the darkened curtain, his hand touching the brown envelope, his new-found Bible. The remnants of snow in the yard reflected the light of the first full moon on a Christmas Eve since 1950, and he clearly saw Cathy in her car. Her head rested on her arms on the wheel, bobbing in time to inaudible sobs. He watched, his big, fat heart aching deliciously. She opened the door of her car. She looked a mess, even in the dim light, her hair disheveled, eyes swollen. Her features were distorted, nearly unrecognizably, by the anguish on her face.

Her key of course didn't work in the shiny new lock he'd installed. He watched as the look of bewilderment added to the anguish on her face, then saw her lips moving, calling. Through the windows and the walls, over the crackling of the fire, he couldn't hear a single word of her silent pleas.

It was better than he could have hoped.

So where was the elation? Where was the magnificent sense of satisfaction that Strauss had promised would be his? From outside, Cathy looked at him, looked toward the darkened window and he saw her mouth saying, *George? George? Where will I go?* From upstairs, Ellen spoke again in her sleep, an indecipherable appeal on behalf of her mother. It was that appeal—it was Ellen—that commenced the meltdown.

It had been Ellen, not him, not his cowardice, that had made him leave the restaurant without confronting Cathy and her lover. George thawed at light speed. He was protecting her. He was George Northey the Protector, protecting Ellen and Cathy and his mother, protecting the innocents. His big heart could take them all in; it was big enough to hold everyone. He was larger than all of them, larger than Strauss, larger than Raymond.

When he opened the door, Cathy's face was a mess, a tangle of smeared make-up, confusion and fear. When she spoke, George softly reassured her, he needed to reassure her, and when she hurried to the bathroom, he threw Strauss's brown envelope into the fire.

He led her to the sofa when she returned, and she waited while he brought her a cup of tea. He sat beside her. She leaned against him, her arm reaching across his bulk quite easily, her face on his shoulder, oblivious to the dampness. The scent of evergreen filled the room. They settled back on the sofa to watch the brown envelope curl and turn to black ash, to watch the fire return to a slow crackle and glow. They listened to Ellen, upstairs in her bed, talking in her sleep. She carried on a long, lively conversation, happy, excited, and unintelligible.

George's heart had never been fuller. It was bursting at the seams.

Wilda Wingard had long since forgiven George for his transgressions against her groceries. But what she could never forgive him for was his apology, coming as it did from beyond the grave.

Not long after he'd mangled her bread and sweated on her tomatoes, she'd read his obituary in the paper. His big, fat heart had attacked him, and Wilda had thought, *What a pity*, nothing more, as she hadn't known the young man well. Weeks passed, George Northey never entering her mind again. Then Elva Plotner, her neighbor at the King George Apartments, came over to visit, and noticed the red light blinking on her phone.

"You have a message," Elva said.

"I do?" Wilda's magnified eyeballs got bigger behind the thick lenses of her glasses. "I thought that just meant the phone was on." The phone was fairly new, a gift from her only son's widow, who lived in Kentucky.

Elva showed her where the Play button was, and pressed it.

"Wilda," said the voice on the phone, "this is George Northey. I just wanted to call you and tell you how sorry I am. I sure didn't mean to scare you. I guess I just had some stuff on my mind and I wasn't thinking about what I was doing. I feel real bad about your bread. I promise to be more careful. Okay? See you later."

Wilda, knowing that George had been dead for several weeks, was afraid. More than afraid, she was indignant. What right had a dead man to call her and apologize for mangling her bread? Who did he think he was? What was he trying to do? Patiently, Elva explained that the message must have been there since Christmas Eve, and, ever so slowly, Wilda came around, began to understand. But still she didn't like it. She had no use at all for technology, never much cared for any of the new-fangled gadgets and gizmos that had thrust themselves into her life. And she never, ever, trusted that telephone, nor the memory of George Northey, again.

ALL ABOUT HEARTS

One last sniffle, one last dab of tissue, a deep breath, and she's ready. If she didn't have to go, she might just sit in the car and cry all night. She gets out. The Christmas lights are off, the house dark. Good. Fitting. Moonlight glistens off the roof, and she wishes she could turn it off as well. It's the first full moon on a Christmas Eve in forty-six years, George told her, since 1950, before any of them—her, George, Steven—were even born. She wishes she'd never been born. She wishes none of them had ever been born. All she wants to do is go to the bathroom, and go to sleep. Surely, she's all cried out by now. But the front door is locked, which makes a train wreck of her resolve, and as she gropes for her key, she notices the new lock glowing like a full moon above the doorknob. Her key doesn't work.

George has changed the lock. *George has changed the lock*? He's there, at the living room window, peeking through the curtain like an assassin, a big, fat teddy-bear of an assassin.

Her impulse is to leave, to find Steven, or maybe not, since she and Steven have just broken up, since she and Steven breaking up was the reason for the tears that kept her a prisoner in her car for the last half hour. Maybe go to her mother's then, maybe to her girlfriend Diane's. But she has to pee too badly—damn the champagne. She has no choice. Frowning at the window she says, "George? George! I have to *go*."

That's all it takes. George, the teddy-bear assassin, crumbles like one of his frosted cupcakes. He opens the door with a broken-hearted look of defiance, guilt and love.

She stares at him hard. "Why did you change the lock?" She and Steven have been careful, but she wonders . . . is George suspicious?

He looks away. "Somebody's been breaking into houses all over town," he says, "stealing Christmas presents." This is news to Cathy. Saying nothing, she hurries to the bathroom.

She pees, and cries a few leftover tears. Surely the tears must be gone. Back in the hallway, she hears Ellen, their little girl, upstairs, garbling in her sleep. George is on the sofa in the living room, before the fire. "Aren't you going to bed?" she says. "Santa won't come while you're still up." He looks at her. What she likes about George—she loves him, she supposes, though far differently from how she loves Steven—is the way he makes her feel beautiful when he looks at her. He's a large man, the sheer size of him contradicting the naked, selfless way he hangs on her every word. There are two kinds of people in the world, she thinks, people who live their lives, and people who watch other people live their lives. She and George. She goes and sits beside him to thank him for watching. She cuddles close against the bulk of him, and together they watch the fire turning slowly to embers. She reaches for him.

"Merry Christmas," she says, her hand on his pants. When he's ready she climbs on him, and slowly they make love. Because of his weight she usually takes the top, a position she'd tried only once before George, without much luck; Marvin Kaderly, the boy she'd gone with in college, Vice-President of the Young Republicans, hadn't much cared for the lack of control. But when she tried the position with Steven, it was thrilling, like riding a wild Mustang; with George she's plodding along atop a friendly old draft horse.

A perfect night for plodding. George is loving and grateful, crying into her chest. Cathy wonders if he can feel Steven, feel where Steven has been inside of her, wonders if George can taste Steven on her mouth, and, as she's wondering, she decides that as soon as they're finished, she'll tell him. She'll make the break with Steven clean and complete, make the fresh start with George honest and open, tell him about the affair she's been having with Steven, the affair they decided this evening to end, when Steven convinced her it could only end in heartbreak, and that the hearts it would break would be those of the innocent, George and Ellen.

When they're done, Cathy embraces the soft mountain of man who is her husband. Now. In the afterglow. "I have something to tell you," she whispers.

George pulls her closer. "What?"

And Cathy, squirming a little, subtly, so as not to hurt his feelings, trying to seem to be wiggling closer, but in reality trying to distance herself from his sweaty armpit, says, "Mother's having a Christmas party Saturday. She wants us both to come."

She's up at six next morning, her head aching badly, but she wouldn't miss her little girl opening presents. Ellen rips through them, gift after gift, littering the living room in the glow of the Christmas tree lights. She and George have overindulged her, mostly at George's insistence, although Cathy was easily persuaded; overindulgence is what Christmas is all about. Her parents showered her with gifts all her life—they still do—and George has as well, outfits and jewelry, a George Foreman Grill, expensive wine, a new lamp she'd been admiring in the window of Bartley's Furniture on Main Street. A touch turns it on and off. She wasn't as generous with George, but that's the nature of the provider—to provide, not to be provided for. And since for the other three hundred and sixty-four days of the year those roles are reversed, Cathy was content to let the natural order prevail on Christmas. George couldn't be happier. One of Ellen's presents is a blackboard, upon which he wrote a message from Santa about what a good girl she's been; he wrote it with his left hand, as if Ellen might be able to identify his handwriting. The little girl hurries from one package to the next, ribbons, paper and giggles flying, and Cathy, for an hour, is there. Then she remembers Steven.

George sits on the sofa beside her. Ellen looks up, jealous, and comes running, her stuffed Barney bouncing behind her, jumping up to get in on the hug. Her knees are sharp and careless, her squirming hard to cuddle. She looks up, alarm on her round little face. "Mommy?" She reaches up, touches Cathy's wet cheek. Cathy hadn't realized she was crying. George hadn't noticed it either.

George says, "Something wrong?"

Ellen says, "May kismas, Mommy?"

"Very merry, sweetie," Cathy says. "Don't you two know that girls cry when they're happy?" And she grabs her little girl and tickles her, and Ellen rolls to the floor laughing and giggling amidst the holiday litter.

She simply has to get out of there. Everything in the house reminds her of Steven. Everything, everywhere she looks—

the butternut tea table, the cluster of pictures on the wall in the den, the formation of cookie jars lined up on the soffit in the kitchen. Why they remind her of Steven she's not sure, since Steven has never been within blocks of her house, but she guesses it's because she's thought of him just about every minute of every day, at every place she's been for the past six months. Since she hasn't been to her mother's that often, it might be better there.

Her mother's house is elegant, expansive, situated on a deep, wooded lot overlooking Hartsgrove, far more substantial than her and George's simple ranch. It's the house where Cathy grew up. It's pre-Steven.

Her parents are in the kitchen; in the living room, the presents sit unwrapped beneath the tree in orderly fashion, the wrapping paper having been neatly discarded, in stark opposition to the chaos on the floor of her own living room. Her father, a tall, lanky man, prone to winks and leers, is standing over the stove, the smell of sizzling bacon filling the room. "Hi, Sweetie—where's Ellen?" he says.

"They'll be up later," Cathy says. "I wanted to get a head start."

"Check this out," her father says. "Gloria, man the pan!"

"Man your own damn pan," says Cathy's mother, looking up from her coffee in the breakfast nook.

"Check this out," her father says to Cathy, leading her to the living room. From beneath the tree, he retrieves a golf club. "Look what your mother got me."

"That's nice," Cathy says. Her father has dozens of golf clubs.

"Wait," he says. He assumes a golfing stance, waving his new club, addressing an imaginary ball. "Now say I hit a bad shot and I'm stuck in the rough. What do I do? Hack away? Chop my way out? No problemento." He turns the club in his hands and twists open the head, then lowers it again, presses a button on the shaft, and a buzzing commences. "Check it out—a weed whacker!"

"Jerry!" says her mother from the nook. "You're going to gouge the floor!"

"It's the Big Daddy!" her father says, laughing, buzzing the carpet. "Is it any wonder I love that woman?"

Cathy looks at her mother. Gloria stares back over her glasses, examining her daughter. She takes her glasses off. "My God—you look awful."

"Thank you, Mother."

"You look as though you're retaining water in your face."

Cathy is ambushed by a sudden attack of tears. "Nice move, dear," her father says, shutting off his Big Daddy. "She isn't retaining it now."

"All I said was—"

Cathy rushes to the bathroom. Is it harder than she thought it would be, or is she weaker than she thought she was? She misses Steven so much. Her mother knocks. "Cathy? What's the matter with you, young lady? It's Christmas."

Cathy opens the door, face dry but puffy. "I'm fine, Mom. It's just my period."

"You're seeing another man, aren't you?"

"No, Mother," says Cathy, unsurprised by the accusation. *I broke up with him last night*, she doesn't say. She says, "I am not seeing another man. You are wrong."

Gloria stares; there's a certain grit in the way she maintains eye contact that belies her surface elegance. She's aging well, her mother; of course Gloria does everything well. Cathy resembles her, a shorter, wider version with a complexion less perfect. Gloria's hair is raven-colored, while Cathy's is still the color of straw that's been left too long in the barn. She is not the natural beauty her mother was—or still is. Cathy blinks first. "You have a daughter," Gloria says. "A beautiful little girl. Exactly how you accomplished that I'm not certain, given the material you had to work with."

"Mother. I did not come up here to be insulted."

"I'm not insulting you, dear. I'm insulting George."

"Oh." She should rally to George's defense. But George is big, fat, without guile and is, to boot, a stock boy at the Golden Days Supermarket, his antiques business having gone under. Not easily defensible.

"At any rate," says Gloria, "I was talking about Ellen. Do you know what a divorce would do to that sweet little thing?"

A shiver of ennoblement creeps up Cathy's spine at the thought of her sacrifice. "Yes, of course. I do."

"Let's take it outside," her father calls from the living room, the Big Daddy purring again, "and see how it works in its native habitat."

She met Steven Charles at a seminar on a hot summer morning in the Seneca Room of the Erie Ramada Inn. They're both real estate agents, she in Hartsgrove, he in Roseville, twenty-two miles west on I-80, toward Ohio. He was—is—five years younger than she, thin and wiry, with unruly dark hair and a face full of twinkles and grins. She was particularly taken by the neatly pressed pleats on the front of his khaki pants.

There are things she loves about George: his personality mostly—especially his bald sincerity, his energy, his devotion to Ellen. Sex with him, though, is not one of the things she loves. Before Steven it hadn't much mattered, for she'd never thought of herself as a sexy creature; with Steven, however, the attraction was so instant and physical it felt like instinct. When he touched her hand reaching for his packet next to hers that first morning in Erie, she felt a surge that took her breath away.

Their rendezvous revolved exclusively around sex and eating, the two most physical of endeavors. Often at the same time. At first, during the hot days of summer and early autumn, they met in motels, bringing food, silly food, gourmet cheeses, hot sausage hoagies with roasted peppers, fried chicken, bunches of grapes, cookies and bottles of champagne; pepperoni sticks were always good for a few lewd laughs. They ate and made love for hours. If hours weren't available, they met at nice restaurants for lunch—sometimes dinner—and made love in one of their cars afterwards, often on Skyline Drive overlooking Hartsgrove. Then, when the weather began to turn colder, she thought of the antiques shop.

Long since closed, Northey's Antiques was George's father's business, then George's for a while, before it withered on the vine. It was a going concern when her father-in-law owned it, but after he died, it did too; George simply isn't a businessman. It occupies a converted gas station—*filling stations* they called them in those days—on the west end of Main Street, the less commercial end. *Filling station* was the appropriate term when she and Steven were there. Full service was all the mode. The ambiance, stilted and ghostly at first, grew comfortable in the mellowness of old wood, the artifacts of leisure and ease, the creature comforts of other ages.

Usually she parked near Himes Funeral Parlor, half a block down. Steven would park on the other end of Main Street, and they'd arrive separately, making their ways discreetly to the back door, hidden by the laurel thicket alongside the building.

"What took you so long?" she would say, hugging him beside the slat-back rockers.

Steven allowed his eyes to adjust to the dim, musty interior. Then he grinned. "You didn't start without me, did you?"

Laughing, Cathy threw her underwear in his face.

In the bay area were half a dozen beds. George's father displayed them complete with mattresses and springs, covered with old quilts and spreads, also for sale. Steven and Cathy tried each bed in turn, making love in the dusty sunlight from the windows high on the old doors that would never creak open again.

One day, cuddling afterwards, Steven said, "I wonder why they don't have one of those things over this bed."

Cathy bit. "One of what things?"

"You know . . . that old-fashioned thing they used to hang over the bed?

"A canopy?"

"No, no," said Steven. "That was *under* the bed." He was impish, corny. The old Maytag in the corner with the wringer he was certain was the one in which his grandma had got her tit caught. He was a natural-born liar, one of the things Cathy loved.

Main Street is the pride of Hartsgrove, Pennsylvania. *Historic Hartsgrove.* A wide street with brick sidewalks and vintage streetlamps, it's lined with two- and three-story Victorian buildings of brick and stone, with elaborate wooden cornices. On the north side in the middle sits the red brick Court House, four giant clocks at the top of its tall tower, each displaying a different time to the four corners of town. Half a block down on the other side of the street, in the storefront of a lesser building is Sadie's Beauty Shop, where her girlfriend Diane does Cathy's nails once a week. Three blocks in the other direction—not far enough—is Northey's Antiques.

Dropping a quarter in the meter, she avoids looking down the street, avoids the antiques shop even in her periphery. Her normal nail appointment is Wednesday, but Wednesday—yesterday—was Christmas, so she's a day late.

She's anxious to have her nails redone; these are the same nails that touched Steven, a constant reminder. She's holding up. She hasn't cried since yesterday evening, when the mashed potatoes George heaped on his plate reminded her of the pillow Steven heaped beneath her hips.

"These don't look too bad," says Diane, examining Cathy's nails on the tabletop. The week before, she painted them for Christmas, red and green with gold glitter. "Maybe we should just do a trim and touch-up."

"Get rid of 'em," Cathy says.

"Bah, humbug," Diane says. She's a big-boned girl with a bulging blouse and dirty blond hair, a shade dirtier than Cathy's. They've been friends since seventh grade. She asks Cathy how her Christmas was. Cathy says don't ask. They chat as Diane applies polish remover. "What color do you want?"

Cathy's first thought is her favorite mood polish, turquoise and pearl, but she remembers wearing that with Steven at the Day's Inn in Harmony Mills. Baby blue and pink she wore when they went to dinner at the Cranberry Mall; they were stained glass the first day she met him in Erie last summer. He commented how pretty they were, how unusual. "Do you have anything new? Any suggestions?"

"You've had 'em all, girlfriend."

Steven calls her girlfriend. *Called* her girlfriend. "Something plain then, I don't care. Plain old pink."

"What's the matter?"

"*Nothing's* the matter." Blinking, she realizes she's crying again.

"Aren't we in a mood," Diane says.

"It's my period." Cathy sees a man outside beyond the big backwards letters spelling *Sadie's*; it isn't Steven, but the man has two arms, two legs, dark hair and a tan jacket. It might have been Steven. Steven has walked down that sidewalk. Cathy sobs.

"This your first period?" says Diane.

Cathy yanks her hand back, putting her head down, sobbing louder. Sadie calls over, "For God's sake, try another color."

Cathy raises her head. "Black—paint 'em *black.*"

Diane retrieves Cathy's hand, massages it. "Is Ellen all right?" Cathy nods, snuffling. "George?" Another nod. "Did you break up with your boyfriend or something?" Cathy freezes in mid-snuffle. Diane says, "Did you think nobody ever saw you two sneaking in and out of the antiques shop?"

Cathy says, "Yes," with a whimper, a nod, another sob.

"Yes, you thought nobody saw you, or yes, you broke up with your boyfriend?"

"Yes," is a pitiful squeak. So Diane knows. Good. Cathy had been dying to tell her. It might help. Once it's out of her system, no longer pent up inside, then surely the tears would stop. Between snuffles and sobs she tells her friend about Steven, how she met him, how they fell in love, the things they did; then, the end, how on Christmas Eve in the Holiday Inn after champagne and orgasms, they decided, finally, they had simply met and fallen in love too late, that the risk of hurting George and Ellen was too great.

Diane looks up from the clear base coat she's applying. "So, let me get this straight. You decided to sacrifice your own happiness for George and Ellen?"

Cathy nods, sniffs.

"That doesn't sound like you at all."

A sneak attack from her closest friend, wielding the most unjust of all weapons: the truth. Cathy sobs even harder, tears and snot both flying at once. Diane pats her hand. "But at least you're handling it like a real trouper."

She hoped her session at Sadie's was the end of it. Tears threaten again that evening, however, when Ellen, scotchtape in her hand and mischief on her mind, looks at her with a twinkle in her eye that resembles Steven's.

He's there, constantly, like a low-grade fever. There's no escape. She once read about a man who hiccupped for fifty years. Maybe she's condemned to cry that long. A freak of nature. Steven is with her as she sits on the sofa with her unread magazine watching George take down the Christmas tree as Ellen scatters checkers on the butterscotch carpet.

Do you know what a divorce would do to that sweet thing? Concentration creases Ellen's face as she tries to stack the checkers, having little luck on the uneven surface of the carpet. George whistles a Christmas carol, even as he dismantles the season. Christmas is over; time to move on. If only it were that easy, moving on. Ellen climbs on the sofa to rest against her mother. Cathy snuggles her close, looking down at the wispy blond hair. George glances over, trying not to smile too broadly.

Ellen would survive. George is the one who wouldn't.

Friday morning Cathy has an appointment to show the Freeman cottage to the Henrys, a young couple in the market for their first house. They've both taught at Hartsgrove High for three years, and Janice Henry is pregnant with their first. They're excited, and naïve. Janice suggests moving the bathroom upstairs, to the opposite side of the house, turning the present bathroom into a sewing room, and Tim imagines remodeling the six-foot, dirt-floored cellar into a family room. Cathy is counting her seven percent.

In the empty living room sunbeams slant through the naked window, illuminating a bright rectangle of hardwood floor, around which they stand. "Oh, I just love it," Janice says.

"It's in our range," says Tim, trying to be cool.

"Don't you think it's just perfect for us?" says Janice, beaming toward Cathy.

Cathy rushes sobbing from the room.

◆   ◆   ◆

In Memorial Park, at the bottom of Hartsgrove where the creeks converge, a skating rink sits between the dormant baseball fields. From the car Cathy and her mother watch George and his father-in-law skating with Ellen.

"I knew it," Gloria says.

"I was *not* lying." Tears cool on Cathy's cheek. "When you asked me, I'd already broken up with him." From the corner of her eye, she sees her mother shaking her head.

"Is he married?"

"No!" She's indignant her mother would even think she'd see a married man, would violate the sanctity of marriage vows, though this particular indignity quickly begins to melt. They watch the skaters—her father, George and Ellen are the only three out on this frosty, sunny Saturday morning—and Cathy is thankful they're there for the watching; confession is easier without her mother's eyes prying the lid off her conscience.

"Did you want to have his baby?"

"George's?"

"No, not George's," Gloria says. "That other fellow's—Steven's."

"No. Of course not."

"Of course not? You had sex with him, didn't you?" Cathy says nothing. Gloria says, "What do you think the purpose of sex is?"

"The purpose of making love is to be as close to somebody as you can possibly be." Cathy is proud of this response. "It's the highest expression of your love."

"The purpose of sex is to perpetuate the species. Remember when you were little, those two dogs in the yard your father threw water on? Do you think they were expressing their love?"

"Did you and daddy only have sex once? You only had one child."

From the corner of her eye, she sees her mother glance sharply. "That is none of your business, young lady." She looked back to the skaters. "We tried to have more."

"Yeah. I sometimes heard you trying."

"You might have heard your father, but you never heard me. Your father, God love him, is essentially a pig. Like most men."

Ellen falls down hard on her padded bottom; her grandfather helps her up, stooping awkwardly on his skates. Cathy remembers him helping her up like that, with a word of encouragement, a good-natured laugh, and she doesn't want to hear this, another attack on her father by her mother; but she doesn't want to fight with Gloria, either. She's too tired. She wants her mother's understanding, her support. "There's a big difference," Gloria says. "Any thinking person knows the difference between being in love and being in heat. I should think you, of all people, would know, after Lester Knapp."

Lester Knapp again. Tears gather for another assault. "Mom . . . I'm trying. I'm trying to get over him, but I can't. We just didn't want to hurt George or Ellen." Cathy reaches for her mother's hand, but her mother, apparently unaware, moves it at the same time to the top of the steering wheel. George glides close, bowing and mugging, his cheeks a fiery red.

"That man is a heart attack waiting to happen," Gloria says.

Cathy's heard it a million times. "He's on a diet, I think."

"That's the only reason you broke it off with this other man? For George and Ellen?"

"Yes. Of course." Another noble sniffle.

"Cathy, that's just not like you at all. Blow your nose."

When she was sixteen, Lester Knapp knocked her up. Lester was a skinny farm boy with big ears who warmed the bench for the Hartsgrove Red Ramblers basketball squad. She'd been attracted by his shyness, into which she'd read—mistakenly, as it turned out—dignity and depth. It was a year or two after Cathy's father had quit his job working for Gloria's father—Zimmerman Gas and Coal—and had taken a job in West Virginia as a branch manager for the competition. He had an apartment near Morgantown, coming home only on weekends, as he does to this day. Cathy missed her father, but the arrangement seemed to suit her parents fine.

She helped Lester with his homework in the basement family room. It was during her mother's piano phase, after the ceramics, after crafts, before painting, in which she still dabbles. One spring evening on the shag carpet listening to "Clair de Lune" over and over again, listening for the piano to stop, Cathy became pregnant.

She turned to her mother as her last resort. Her girlfriend Diane hadn't been helpful, lecturing Cathy about rubbers. Lester Knapp she never told. The truth about his shyness had surfaced. Her mother's reaction was more disgust than anger; Cathy was relieved. Disgust was comfortably subtle; anger would have magnified the terror. Two weeks later, Gloria took her to a country clinic far from Hartsgrove for an abortion.

Doctor Deerlick. She doesn't remember his name, but she remembers the deer lick, and every time she thinks of that day, it's Doctor Deerlick. She remembers white bristly hair and loose jowls, a stern expression that mirrored her mother's.

She remembers fear, discomfort, the table hard and cold, and when she looked through the window, the long lawn behind the clinic sloping down to the trees reminded her of her parents' camp—a country home, really, large and well-appointed, with an in-ground pool—where they spent holidays and weekends in the deep woods north of

Hartsgrove. Through the clinic window, she saw a white object near the tree line. A deer came out of the woods, making its way gingerly toward the thing. The doctor looked, following her gaze. "That's my salt lick," he said. "Deer love it. I've counted as many as eight of them back there at once, licking away, all taking turns."

As she watched, the deer reached the white square and began licking, head bobbing gently. Feet high and cold in the stirrups, vulnerable and frightened, Cathy felt quite susceptible to the idea of compassion. *How very kind*, she thought.

Between her knees, she saw the doctor smile his only smile of the day. "Instant venison," he said.

The steeple of the Catholic church on Irishtown hill is visible from all over town, a tarnished needle piercing a soft blue sky. Cathy sees it, part of the sweeping view of Hartsgrove, through the window above her mother's sink, where she stands washing radishes. She's never stared at the steeple before, seen it only in passing, every day, a piece of growing up, woven into the fabric of her life. Now the sight of it causes her eyes to tear again.

Beside her, her mother slices the radishes. Gloria's elegant hands are not made for the task and the slices are crooked, too thick. In the backyard, her father plays with his Big Daddy. The lawn is spotted with bare patches, an ugly brown leopard skin where he's whacked around teed-up golf balls, before whacking them away toward the trees along the far side of the yard. "I guess you made a big hit with that present," Cathy says.

"He's ruining my lawn."

"But he's having fun."

Gloria places her knife firmly on the countertop. "He is such a little boy. But aren't they all? Little boys with their little toys."

Cathy's chuckle fails her. She suddenly misses her father, and missing her father is missing Steven, and the melancholy ripples out, random thoughts of heartbreak and loss assaulting her from every direction. Turning off the water, Gloria takes her wrist, looks in her face, reaches up and wipes away her daughter's tear. Cathy is seven again. She moves close to her mother, embraces her, holds her; she feels her mother stiffen for an instant before her arms come up in a loose embrace. They stand for a moment in an awkward hug. Gloria says, "Do you want me to get Milford? I think he's up in the attic."

Cathy steps back, wiping her cheek with the back of her hand. "Don't you think I'm a little old for a teddy bear?" Besides, Milford isn't in the attic; Milford is at home, at Cathy's, waiting on the shelf in her closet.

Squeezing her wrist Gloria says, "Go home. Get some rest. I don't want you to come to my party tonight. You're in no condition to socialize—I can just imagine you breaking down at the height of the festivities, dripping tears, or something worse, into the pâté."

At home, Cathy retreats to the den, shutting the blinds against the bright afternoon. George and Ellen have gone to see *101 Dalmatians* in Harmony Mills. Taking the red Afghan and a box of Kleenex, she curls on the sofa, face buried in the back cushions. Having not slept well for the past three nights, she's soon dozy and dreamy. What would Steven be doing at this moment? She can't imagine. Try as she may, she can't picture him beyond memory, as though he ceased to be after Christmas Eve. Then she sees him throwing a football to a boy—who the boy is, or why Steven should be playing with him, she can't muster the energy to imagine. She feels oppressed, put upon. Why? She's certainly not the only woman to ever have an affair, to ever become entangled in complications of the heart. There's Princess Di. Madame

Bovary. Helen of Troy. Mary Lou McAfoose down the street with her famously blackened eye. Cathy drifts. Imagining all the women in history who've ever had affairs: flappers, Victorian women, colonial women, Renaissance women, medieval women, cave women, in all their darkened nooks and hideaways, shedding undergarments from beneath bustles and gowns, robes and rags. In her dream, she sees the human race from above, far above, random particles shooting through time and space, constantly bumping into and off of one another by chance, occasionally clinging together. Before bouncing free again and far away.

Lurching back from the verge of sleep. It's *not* like her, this sacrifice thing. Chilled by the coldness of the truth, she pulls the Afghan tighter. Diane was right; Gloria was right. If it was not her idea, then whose idea was it? Steven. It must be him; Steven was the noble one.

She sleeps. She loves George. But she loves Steven more. Simple as that.

She sleeps. The sofa sinks. George beside her.

She can make out only his hulking silhouette. Dark. How long has it been?

"I can't stand seeing you like this," he whispers. "Do you want to go back to him?"

She blinks. "You knew?"

The shadow nods. "I just want you to be happy."

"Where's Ellen?"

"At your mother's. At the party."

In the scant light she can barely see his wide open face, a face incapable of hiding the emotion behind it, his eyebrows arching, defying gravity. In the shadows his big cheeks glisten. Desire rises like a bubble. She takes his hand and pulls it to her ribs, sliding it up to lift her breast, the way Steven did. In the shadows his hands become Steven's, his mouth the mouth of her lover.

Sex with George had been infrequent and obligatory. The best was the night Ellen was conceived. George had been dancing all evening, showing off at a party, and afterward felt pain in his chest. The pain grew, his color draining, he was sweating, bald head glistening, and they feared the worst. She rushed him to the emergency room, where indigestion was diagnosed. Back home, she seduced him on the floor in the den, insisting and pleading by turns, threatening to kill him if he ever tried to die on her again.

He was, after all, a heart attack waiting to happen.

The fire is ignited; there's no turning back. Cathy is determined to make him her lover. The sex is long and hard and wonderful, from the den to the hall to the bedroom; time and again she pulls him back from the brink, urging him on. George becomes inspired, wondrous, proving himself, venturing into new territory, positions and durations previously unimagined. He's agile and light as a flame, consuming her, licking her everywhere at once. He takes ownership, something he's never done before, something Steven always did. George fights through exhaustion and beyond, to another plateau, a second wind, a third, surpassing Steven, becoming the lover his wife has always dreamed of.

Finally, he succumbs with a soft moan. Cathy kisses his sweaty forehead, his sweaty cheek. She waits, holding her breath, holding and holding, as George becomes heavier and heavier, and she remembers the legend of the two little girls who vanished in the woods near her parents' camp before Cathy, or the camp, were ever born. They'd been remembered, their ghosts imagined, around many a camp fire. They'd gone berrying in the woods near their grandfather's farm, never to be seen again, and whenever Cathy misbehaved, her father, with a wag of his long, lean finger, would threaten to take her berrying.

Finally Cathy squirms free, sidles away and goes to the bathroom. Washing her hands, she splashes water on her face, looking at herself in the mirror for a long time, into the eyes that are dry, and, just as she suspected, innocent. George lies peacefully on the bed, past sorrow, immune to heartbreak. George, big, fat, sweet, noble, puppy-dog of an assassin, has given his all. George has loved his life away.

It's Sunday evening before all the arrangements are made, all the details seen to, before she finally has a chance to call Steven. She grieves for George and his big, broken heart, but George is gone now, and life goes on. She's learned from George how to move on. There are proprieties and limits of course, which she doesn't care to explore; all she knows is she loves Steven, he loves her, and since they sacrificed that love for the sake of someone now gone, it only stands to reason they should be together. The very logic of it is so sound it renders the outcome unlikely. It's the eyes of that unlikeliness she's poised to attack, to scratch out with her long, black fingernails.

She calls him on his cell. He's surprised to hear from her, shocked by the news. Of course he wouldn't have heard, not in Roseville, a town away.

"I can't talk right now," he whispers. "Meet me."

On Skyline Drive, overlooking Hartsgrove, she waits; it will take Steven half an hour at best, but she couldn't wait at home where she might have been held captive by more condolences. Overhead, much of the moon is missing since Christmas Eve. The lights of the town below are abetted by a scattering of Christmas lights, and she tries to imagine the four thousand souls hunkered there, living their lives, eating, sleeping, watching television, making love, but she can't picture a single one of them. George she can picture, in the dark stillness of the funeral home basement, until the headlights of Steven's car come bouncing toward her on the rutted dirt road below.

Later she thinks it would have been to her credit if they'd had sex before Steven's confession, but that isn't the way that it happens. After she climbs into the front seat beside him, even before they kiss, he tells her. He's married, has been for three years. A son, two, and a little girl, one. Cathy of course has known all along, though only now does she realize it.

"You *lied* to me?"

"No. I didn't." He touches her chin. "You never asked."

Her hand falls to his lap. He slides his seat back. She knows a lie when she hears one, even an untold lie, but any significance the lie might hold is lost in the glow of the moon, the glow of the town, and the glow of the dashboard lights. This is how life must be lived, in the moment, and this is all she's ever wanted, to be held.

The viewing is at Himes Funeral Parlor on Main Street. The stream of family and friends swells to a torrent with more distant family and friends, acquaintances, distant acquaintances, and even the curious, those who think they might have known a man called George Northey. The fat man is fondly remembered. Cathy feels like a genuine widow.

They place a chair in the receiving line for George's mother, too frail to stand, and tears wash her round, wrinkled face. Ellen isn't there, having been left with the sitter; when they told her her daddy had gone away, her face melted into tears. Gloria dabs at her makeup, cursing the running mascara. Even Cathy's father's eyes glisten. George's belly protrudes above the coffin rim. Four whispered syllables—*only forty*—roll around and around the room. Not a dry eye in the house. Except for Cathy's.

Diane hugs her. When Diane cries, her face gets twisted and ugly, probably why she seldom cries. George's friend,

Strauss the butcher, is next in line. Strauss is short, wiry and tough, a Pittsburgh Steelers fan whom one would accuse of softness only at great personal peril. Even Strauss' eyes betray signs of dampness.

Cathy's face is dry as chalk.

"So sorry for your loss," says a small, wide lady dressed in blue jeans, her eyes brimming behind white-rimmed glasses. "Was your husband one of the Slabtown Northeys?"

"I have no idea," Cathy says.

This sets off Gloria, hugging Strauss the butcher, and a chain reaction of sobs ensues. Cathy escapes to the front porch of the funeral parlor, the tune already commencing in her head: *Slabtown Northey, sing this song—do-dah, do-dah.* Walking to the far corner of the porch she stands, her back to the door and all the wet-faced mourners, and gazes down Main Street. At the stop light on Valley, a car stalls, a horn beeps. When she was little her father used to let her shift. When they went for milk and bread, he'd guide her hand on top of the gearshift knob. Half a block down on the other side of the street is Northey's Antiques— painful to look at, impossible to look away from. Now it's dark and cold, but in the morning the sun will burst through the high bay windows, slanting in on all the colorful quilts on all the creaky, delightful old beds. Cathy savors the sensations caused by the sight and the memories—and the anticipation—including the dampness between her legs. The Pavlovian effect strikes her funny. Blinking her bone-dry eyes she has to laugh at the irony of the inverted dampness, and the laughter grows until her shoulders are shaking with it, and she can feel them staring, all the other mourners, staring at the grieving widow, alone in the corner, convulsing with sobs.

Slabtown Northey, sing this song—do-dah, do-dah. It's good to be alive.

DEAD MAN'S FLOAT

1. Prologue

The car was parked at the edge of the Maple Street Elementary School lot, in the farthest corner from the building itself, near the playground. It was coated by a dusting of snow from the night before, making it difficult to even tell what color it was. The kid didn't think much about it, or wonder why someone would have left their car parked overnight in an elementary school parking lot. He was eleven going on seventeen. His nickname was Chip, for the front tooth he'd broken in a skateboarding accident, and he carried that same skateboard under his arm—the snow on the streets made it hopeless to ride—scarcely glancing at the car on his way to the playground. He was in a foul mood. His little sister was sick, again, and his mother and father were falling all over each other bringing her this and that, taking her temperature, giving her lozenges and ice cream. None of his buddies were around. He was too old for the playground, but what the hell. Nobody else was around except for some little kid, some dweeb, a fourth-grader he thought, who was swinging on a swing so high it looked as if his glasses might fly right off his head. There was nothing else to do. He was bored. The dweeb's glasses were clear-framed, geeky, and too big for his face. Chip climbed up, took a spin down the circular slide, snow powder flying.

The dweeb stopped swinging. "Are you going skate-boarding?" he said.

"Du-uh," Chip said. "Too much snow."

"My mom won't let me have one."

"Too bad. So sad. That's a crying shame."

"So, do you want to be friends?"

"I already have friends. Get some friends your own age." Chip doubted he could.

The dweeby kid thought about it for a minute, then his face lit up. "I know something you don't know," he said.

This annoyed Chip, who heaved a shoulder-shrugging sigh and climbed back up the slide ladder. He glanced at the dweeb, who was staring up at him from the swing, clutching the chains like a klutz, an expectant look on his face, his eyeballs as big as his glasses. "What?" Chip said, as bored as he could possibly be.

"There's somebody in that car," the dweeby kid said.

"What car? That car?" Chip, at the top of the slide, nodded toward the snow-plastered car parked fifty feet away.

"Yep. Some man. He's just sitting in there."

2. Ellen

Her phone woke her, "Clair de Lune," Glory's ringtone, a curious thing—her grandmother, a late sleeper, never called at this hour of the morning. Beside her in bed, her boyfriend, Aaron, gave a snort and a gasp at the sound.

"Glory?" she answered her phone. Her grandmother's name, Gloria, had proved too much for a two-year-old tongue, after *grandma* had been quashed by Gloria. Glory had stuck.

"Ellen," her grandmother said, "have you heard from your mother?"

"No. Not recently." Nor had she been expecting to.

"Neither have I. Not for over a week. She doesn't answer her phone. She's not home."

"Oh dear."

"Just like her," Glory said. "A week before Christmas."

"I'm sure she'll turn up."

"Can you come home? We need to talk."

"We are talking."

"Not on the phone." Glory's voice held little softness, no patience.

Ellen asked her grandmother to hold on for a second. "Excuse me," she said to Aaron, looking up from his pillow damp with drool. He frowned, stretched and unfolded himself from the bed, naked, scratching random areas with skinny, roaming hands. When he'd gone into the bathroom, Ellen told her grandmother that her last exam was that afternoon, she could come home after that. She brushed aside a hint of resentment; while she didn't like being at Glory's beck and call, she realized that humoring her grandmother was a necessary precaution, like a flu shot. Glory was, after all, paying for her college, every dime of it. Her grandmother didn't answer right away. In the dim little bedroom—her off-campus apartment was tiny—a hint of sunshine burst through the window behind her, casting a pink glow on the wall with a silhouette of the Garfield figurine on the sill. She could hear Aaron in the bathroom. The toilet flushed so loudly it might have been in the same room.

"Glory? Are you still there?"

"Come home," Glory commanded. "We'll talk then."

When Aaron returned, Ellen said, "Could you try peeing against the side of the bowl? And maybe not fart till you leave?"

"What?" He was thin, bony shoulders, rolling ribs, and his dark, thick, hair might have been molded from paper mâché. Face lowered, he wiggled his eyebrows at her, a parody of romantic intentions. "Does madam see anything she might like?"

She did. She resisted. "Go. I have things I have to do."

She watched him dress, sitting up in bed, holding the covers up to, but not over, her breasts, hiding what she considered to be her unsexy rolls of flab. Aaron didn't seem to agree with her harsh self-assessment. He seemed, instead, to revel in the abundance of her. She was a large, heavy girl with a beautiful face, eyes the color of twilight. He leaned to kiss her cheek. "Bye—I love you."

"Love you too." She watched him go. Did she love him? Or was it simply a case of affection enhanced by desperation? Did she love him mostly just for loving her? She was water seeking its own level, still trying to arrive at her proper level of confidence and self-esteem. Of her two role models, her mother had far too little of either, her grandmother far too much of both.

Alone in the quiet, it occurred to her that Glory was also alone in a quiet, albeit much larger, house, having just buried her husband, Ellen's grandfather, only a month before. At the wake, Cathy—Ellen's mother, Glory's daughter—had been the life of the party, drinking, laughing, charming—typical Cathy. Ellen by now had moved beyond believing her mother to be the most charming, mysterious woman in the world, but hadn't yet arrived at the disapproval with which her grandmother clearly regarded her. But that night, at the wake—this realization came to her only now—her grandmother seemed to have been more concerned than annoyed.

When Glory turned the corner from recrimination to concern, maybe it was time to worry.

It was well after dark when Ellen arrived home in the early evening, and she wasn't surprised, after talking with Glory, that the lights were all out in her house—in her mother's house. From the driveway where she lingered for a few moments, moonlight glistened off the roof, off the remnants of snow in the yard. Inside, it was hot. Frowning, she turned down the thermostat. She went from room to room, shaking her head, opening doors, switching on lights, switching them off again, not knowing what she was looking for, certain her mother wasn't there. Occasions when Cathy might be sufficiently inebriated to render her oblivious were much rarer nowadays.

Cathy lived alone now that Ellen was away at school. Ellen's father, Cathy's first husband, a man named George, had died years ago, when Ellen was only two. He'd been a big man, whom Ellen couldn't remember, and from whom she'd inherited her size (a constant theme of Glory's). He'd been felled by a heart attack, a heart attack, according to family legend, that had been waiting to happen. Her second marriage, to an older man with shifty eyes and mottled skin, hadn't lasted two years. Ellen had never liked that one, nor many of her mother's other male friends.

The place was messy, just shy of a shambles, a few dirty dishes in the sink—the remains of a meal for one—mail, newspapers, magazines in untidy heaps, soiled clothes overflowing the hamper. Stark contrast to the neatness of Glory's place, though she wondered how much of the contrast was due to the respective natures of her mother and her grandmother, how much due to the fact that Glory had a housekeeper. Ellen lingered a bit longer in her own room, neat and orderly, the way she'd always kept it, untouched by her mother's messiness. A shrine, perhaps? Or just a shut-off room her mother didn't have to worry about cleaning? Looking at her bed with the white headboard adorned with red heart stickers, her small white desk with the gooseneck lamp, the David Beckham poster on the wall—then back to her bed. Something was missing. It took her a moment to name it: her mouse. Her ratty old stuffed mouse, Malachy, frayed, threadbare and gray, with whom she'd grown up, whom she'd long since set aside. When she'd gone off to college, packing, she'd happened across him in the bottom of her chest, rescued him, put him out into the daylight again, propping him on her pillows at the head of her bed to watch over the place while she was gone. Now Malachy himself was among the missing. Had her mother finally thrown him out?

Leaving, she noticed the newspaper. On the sofa, apart from the other papers, it caught her eye because it was there, and because it was open. A Pittsburgh Post-Gazette, a few days old, it was turned to page three of the regional section. Ellen scanned the headlines: a lawsuit, an advisory panel, a DWI arrest, a barn collapse. And one called *Suspicious death.*

> TARENTUM – Police are investigating the death of a man found in his car in an elementary school parking lot Saturday morning by two children playing at a nearby playground. The body has been identified as that of Andrew McAninch, 45, of Tarentum, an audit supervisor for the Pennsylvania Department of Revenue. Police have confirmed the victim died of a gunshot

wound, but are withholding additional information pending the outcome of an investigation. Anyone with any information is asked to call the Tarentum Police Department.

Andrew McAninch. A chill. Ellen had heard the name before. The first iota of worry leaked in. Until now, her mother's escapades, her vanishings for days, even weeks, at a time, had seemed to Ellen to be a natural part of her mother's make-up, something she'd grown up with. Her mother had been born a hippie, apparently (Ellen had only read about hippies), and Ellen, for most of her life, had defended her against Glory's constant chiding. She was afraid she'd inherited more of her grandmother's nature than Cathy's, and she wished sometimes she could be more like the butterfly her mother was.

But butterflies, she must remember, were fragile things.

Glory's house was stone, elegant, expansive, situated on a deep, wooded lot overlooking Hartsgrove, far more substantial than the simple ranch across town where Ellen lived with her mother—or had, before she'd gone away to school. It too was dark.

Glory's cars, a Land Rover and BMW coupe, sat far back in the shadows of the driveway, in front of the stone garage. A glint of moon through skeletons of trees. The dark and the quiet reminded Ellen of the nights, a decade and more ago, when Cathy had brought her, and sometimes her little friends, Halloweening at Glory's. *Halloweening*—a popular, long-standing Hartsgrove sport. Glory normally kept her lights off, pretending no one was home, discouraging trick-or-treaters, whom she equated with beggars. Trick-or-treating, however, was not what Cathy had in mind; she and her youthful accomplices, dressed in black, creeping through the woods, wreaked havoc, soaping windows, corning the porch, toilet-papering the shrubs and trees, until the lights suddenly flashed on, and they made good their giggling escape. And Glory, the next day, afterwards, relating it to Cathy and Ellen, her seething frustration, the hopelessness of the police, the gall of some people, vandalism, criminality.

Though sometimes—again, in hindsight—a certain, knowing look in her eye.

The door was locked. Ellen tapped, then knocked more loudly, and when still no one answered, she let herself in with her key. Called softly. No answer. Glory was sitting in the sunroom, looking out over the lights on the hillsides of the little town. There was light enough from the moon and the snow and the town to see around the room, Glory sitting in the rocker staring out, the ferns in casual array by the walls of windows. "What if I'd thought no one was home?" Ellen said. "What if I'd just driven away?"

"I knew you'd figure it out," Glory said. "You're a smart girl."

"Shall I turn on the lamp?"

"No. Sit."

Ellen found the wicker lounge plush with pillows. "Why are we sitting in the dark?"

"I like it. It gives you a fresh perspective."

"Okay. What's your fresh perspective?"

"I'm very concerned about your mother," her grandmother said.

"That's not fresh. You told me that on the phone."

"Don't be fresh." Glory's rocker gave an impatient squeak. "Your mother, as you know, was crazy about her father—about your grandfather. God knows why. Oh, don't get me wrong, he was a good man, but he was so seldom here for her.

Maybe it was a case of absence making the heart grow fonder, I don't know." For decades, her grandfather had worked in Morgantown, commuting home on weekends. Even after he retired, he'd spent much of his time at his old camp on the river, a derelict old camp that Glory disliked, seldom visited. Ellen had been to the camp only a handful of times herself, with her mother. It was rudimentary, the opposite of his and Glory's house in town, and Ellen remembered mostly being bored while her mother and grandfather talked on the lawn chairs in the weedy yard overlooking a bend in the river, listening to country music, barbequing steaks or pork chops on a rusty old grill. Ellen didn't care for country music. It was just after she'd started high school, and she had better things to do.

"I don't believe you noticed," Glory said, "how very upset she was at his funeral."

"More than the rest of us? Maybe she did get a little drunker. Just drowning her sorrows, so to speak?"

"Drowning her sorrows, sure, but there was no 'just' about it. It was pure desperation. It was a cry for help."

"It was?"

"And perhaps I didn't heed it as well as I should have. After all, I was upset too. He was my husband. I was terribly fond of him too."

"*Fond* of him?"

"Don't be fresh," Glory said. "And now your mother's disappeared. I'm worried."

"Me too. I'm terribly fond of her."

"Don't be fresh." An old-fashioned Gloria glare. "Channel that finely honed wit into thinking of how we might find her."

Ellen handed her the newspaper, the one she'd found on her mother's sofa, folded to the article about the death of Andrew McAninch. "Clue number one?" she said.

Glory sighed. "Let's have a cup of tea," she said, and Ellen followed her into the kitchen, staring down at the smaller old lady, towering over her, feeling gangly and graceless. Glory switched on only the light above the sink and stood reading, leaving the room dim and shadowed. The kitchen of tiles, polished wood and gleaming metal was too broad and barren for Ellen's tastes. She sat at the table in the breakfast nook. Out through the windows, across the gray snow on the dark yard, sat the cars and garage like dead things. Glory rustled the paper to the counter, ran the water and put on the kettle, then turned and came to Ellen. She moved slowly, less determined than she had been just a month before, at her husband's funeral. But her face, as she neared, looked even more beautiful—or was it just the dim light? How many people had told Ellen she had her grandmother's eyes?

"I remember the name," said Glory. "Someone she met in rehab, I think."

Andrew McAninch.

"I remember hearing it too. But I couldn't remember in what context."

They listened to the water start to boil. "Sometimes with your mother," said Glory, "there is no context."

Early next morning, Ellen drove her grandmother's BMW down Route 28 toward Tarentum, Glory her skeptical sidekick. Glory considered it gauche for two otherwise intelligent adults to be traipsing about the countryside playing Nancy Drew—why couldn't she simply *hire* a private detective?—but Ellen thought her grandmother needed her hair messed up, needed an adventure, and Glory acquiesced, reluctantly, skeptically. Glory had talked to family and friends, anyone who might have an inkling as to Cathy's whereabouts. Nothing. Mrs. Altman, Cathy's neighbor, might have seen her car there a day or two ago, but she couldn't be certain.

The police chief, Harold Evans, said he would put out a missing persons bulletin, but Glory could tell he was patronizing her from the moment she told him that Cathy hadn't shown up for their appointment to have their nails done. No one took it seriously. Everyone knew Cathy.

And what would they do when they found her? Another stint in rehab? Every rehab so far had been followed by relapse. Another intervention? Interventions hadn't helped much either, perhaps, Ellen speculated, because of her own less-than-enthusiastic participation. She couldn't entirely condemn her mother's lifestyle, her mother's choices. Didn't Glory often give her cause? And yet she *had* participated. Glory had seen to that.

"I'm still not sure what we hope to accomplish," Glory said.

"Maybe she'll *be* there," said Ellen. In her periphery, Ellen saw Glory shake her head, whether at the unlikelihood of encountering Cathy at the funeral, or at her lingering irritation at Ellen's gadgetry, she couldn't be sure. Ellen knew not only when the funeral was and where, but where Andrew McAninch had lived, the names of his two children, the name of his wife. Or his estranged wife, or ex-wife. The obituary had not listed a wife, just the mother of his children. All of this and more she'd learned on her phone. Glory had refused to believe it was possible. She'd been astonished. More than astonished, she'd been annoyed.

They drove for a while without talking, the radio low, the sun peeking over the hills, past the occasional lonely general store and gas station, the odd farm here and there. It was an hour and a half to Tarentum, a lonely ride, traffic sparse. When an old Beatles song came on, Glory turned it up. Ellen, mildly surprised, glanced at her grandmother singing silently along: *I heard the news today, oh boy . . . four thousand holes in Blackburn, Lancashire . . .* Glory and the Beatles? An odd fit, in Ellen's mind, which associated her grandmother with classical music—"Clair de Lune"—or maybe show tunes. When it was over, Glory turned the volume down again.

"Your mother was never the same after your father died." Ellen glanced again, but Glory was staring into the sky, into the past. "Do you even remember him? No. You wouldn't. You were only, what, two? He was such a big, fat, sloppy man, but he had a good heart, I suppose. Though maybe not—it was his heart, after all, that killed him. You know that already, I'm sure, you've heard it before. But I doubt you know how. He died *in flagrante delicto*—on top of your mother, poor thing. I can't begin to imagine how she even got out from under him. I suppose I shouldn't be telling you this. But you have a right to know. It was that, more than anything, that changed her. Ever since George died on top of her, she has never been the same. Not really."

"Glory—my God. How icky."

"*Icky?* It's true."

"But do you have to tell me?"

"You're a big girl now," Glory said, adding, aside, "thanks to George." Then she said, "Don't you want to know?"

"No," Ellen said. A moment later she said, "Yes."

"Good. You should know what we're looking for." Glory turned the radio off, looking out the window at the countryside coming awake. "Because God only knows what we'll find."

3. Andrew

Immersed, he opened his eyes and it was like staring up at heaven from the inside of a pearl, shimmering opalescence, a pleasant sensation, despite the chlorine in the pool. His heartbeat filled his body, surely filling the length and breadth of the pool, and he wondered if Cathy could feel it as well. Naked, he floated up, breaking the surface, closing his eyes. He couldn't feel Cathy, off adrift on her own somewhere. *Dead man's float.* When they were kids, they used to perform that trick now and then, pretend they were dead, float in the water, limp—*lifeless!*—imagining the awful mourning of parents and friends, the unfathomable idea of a world marching on without them—until they could no longer hold their breath. This, of course, was not a dead man's float. He was on his back. All he had to do was roll gently toward the bottom of the pool, but how could he possibly conjure up the energy to do that? A sound of soft, swishing liquid, and he braced himself, and sure enough, a hand from nowhere saved him, grasping him by what he fondly referred to as his visceral extension.

He'd met her in rehab, Maple Hill Manor, in the spring, the first afternoon he was admitted. He wanted just to bury his head in his pillow and sleep, but the counselor, mean, robotic man, hair perfectly black, perfectly combed, asked him what he thought he was doing, did he think he was at a luxury spa?, and escorted him to his first group session. There sat Cathy in the circle of curious faces, though hers wasn't the first one his eyes settled on. That came later as he stood and told his story—his name was Andrew and he was an alcoholic, his wife had abandoned him and his two children (nearly grown, but needy still), *Gretchen* was her name, flushing their lifetime together down the toilet, and this on top of months of open, flaunted infidelity. And as he studied the circle of deflecting faces, superficially sympathetic, only one was totally absorbed, homing down the lifeline of their locked gazes as if they were the only two in the room, as if his story was for her ears only: Cathy. He knew then, without realizing it, that he was to be her next addiction. And, for a while, it gave him hope, a different kind of hope.

After the session, she came and stuck her face in his, and said, "*Gretchen*? Who names their kid Gretchen anymore?"

"Only the most primitive of tribes," he said.

The face in question was not beautiful, though it had that potential, as if it could have been, as if it had come this close, but detoured into rough-hewn, worn and aging. But the earnest vulnerability with which she presented it more than compensated, and he thought the idea of her face was beautiful, if not the actual artifact. Eyes light blue and cool. They spent every minute they could together for the next three weeks—her last three of five at Maple Hill Manor, his first three of four— and he found himself welcoming her company, found himself more talkative, communicative, than he'd ever been, really, at any time before. Once he confided: had she ever considered ending her life? Cathy gave a scoffing cluck, looking around the room. He was obviously new to rehab, she said. Everyone there considered it every day. It was a given. Hadn't he? Andrew shrugged in reply. His kids must have thought so, he said. They'd taken away his pistol, his .22. The stories of their lives, stories of overcoming and succumbing, again and again, poured out as easily and fragrantly as wine from a bottle. He had a high forehead, fine, sandy hair and outdoorsy good looks, despite his narrow shoulders, even though he'd only dabbled in fishing and hadn't hunted since his father took him into the woods when he was nine. She made him feel handsomer than he was. Chemistry was the word. Spontaneous combustion. And he never asked himself, not in the beginning, how long an accidental fire sparked by spontaneous combustion could burn. The future in fact held little interest for him.

He gave rehab a shot. He tried. He committed himself. He believed that the people running Maple Hill Manor knew what they were doing, or at least were sincere in their efforts, and who was he to hurt their feelings by acting otherwise? Cathy, not so much. He interacted with all the people in the same boat as him, people who purportedly knew what he was going through, he watched the videos, listened to the lectures, participated in the sessions, took his meds like a good boy. Cathy on the other hand, a veteran of rehab, was not only skeptical, but resentful—at having to stand in line for meds she felt she didn't need, at not being able to have her own shampoo (as if, she told him indignantly, she might actually *drink* it), at not being able to read a novel of her own choosing, but instead being expected to read, of all things, the *Bible*. She was not a Bible person, she told him. She didn't like being treated like a child. He, on the other hand, had no problem surrendering his adulthood for a while, putting his life's everyday decisions into the hands of others, knowing what a stew he'd been making of them himself the last few years. His and Cathy's opposing viewpoints became a symbiosis of sorts, keeping them afloat until she was gone. They arranged to meet after he got out.

He was from Tarentum, she from Hartsgrove, so they met near the middle, just south of Harmony Mills. With golden intentions, of course, at a coffee shop. When he walked in, she was waiting. "Don't *you* look rehabilitated," she said. "You're positively glowing." He said, "It's probably just my after-shave," and they sat for a while drinking coffee, snidely commenting on the pretensions of the customers in the shop, their espressos and lattes and laptops, trying on the outside world and their new place within it to see how it fit. They talked about returning to their jobs—she sold real estate, at least part-time, living mostly off the largesse of her mother's inherited wealth (a full-time job in itself, she told him, pushing all her mother's right buttons).

He was nothing so convoluted, just a straight-forward tax auditor for the state of Pennsylvania, due Monday morning at *Joe's Pizz-ahh!* in Johnstonville. They talked about what they'd left behind, wondering how Adolf—their nickname for the plastic-haired counselor who ran the group sessions—was faring with poor Arlon, the pimple-faced kid who got the hiccups every time he spoke in group. Within an hour, they'd checked into the Holiday Inn.

At Maple Hill Manor there'd been no opportunity for privacy, and they made love as if they were twenty again. He was forty-five, she somewhere north of fifty, but when they were finished, they did it again. Then they napped, and then they made love again, but after the third time their reserves were depleted and they knew it. Their naps were used up as well. They had no plan. They heard a car horn outside in the parking lot, a squeal of brakes, and, a moment later, the sound of a child running in the hallway outside their second-floor room.

"Man," he said. "That was close."

"What was?"

"That car. Almost hit that kid."

She frowned. Rolled her eyes. "You are just a little bit nuts."

"Really?" he said. "Would a person a little bit nuts try to steal your nose?" and he did, his hand nabbing at her face, thumb protruding from his fist. "Got it!"

"That's going to cost you," she said, making her move. Clutches, tickles and giggles ensued, two mature, middle-aged adults, and when it was through, they lay on their sides, panting, sweating. He studied her lips, the wry little smile. Remembered those lips so skillfully, gently, assuredly caressing his erection, and he remembered his wife's lips doing the same, for oh so many years, and he pictured his wife's lips doing the same to the erection of a stranger. To the erections of strangers. *Wretched Gretchen*, he murmured, almost involuntarily. That was the name Cathy had bestowed upon her not so very long ago.

"What did you say?" she said.

"I said—" He cocked his hand behind his ear. From the bar downstairs the sound of a song drifted up: *Margaritaville.* "I said, listen—they're playing our song."

Four o'clock in the afternoon, a sunny, hot, summer afternoon. They needed a plan. There was an outdoor patio at the bar overlooking the pool. "God," she said. "Wouldn't a gin and tonic taste delicious right now?"

"Tell you what," he said, their faces inches apart on the pillow, her eyes icy blue. "I'll be your relapse trigger if you'll be mine."

Her eyes misted. "That might be the sweetest thing any man has ever said to me."

She stood in the water beside him as he floated in the pool. A hand beneath his back, steadying him, the other on his genitals, coaxing his penis with gentle tugs to rise above the water. Skinny-dipping had been her idea. An old family tradition, she said. He wondered about the meaning of the remark, but not deeply, only as profoundly as nine hours of bingeing would allow: nine hours of gin and tonics, beer, margaritas of course, a schnapps or two. Water up to her breasts. Pretty breasts for a woman her age, and he was overwhelmed with gratitude that she would show them to him, would allow him the freedom to gaze upon, to touch, to put his lips to her breasts, to indeed open herself up utterly and allow him, another animal, to come into her. So overwhelmed that he began to weep, though the tears were indistinguishable from the pool water on his face. Reflections of light in the darkened glass face of the closed bar, slashed with red neon, slanting rays of light from beside the pool and the parking lot beyond, a celebration of luminescence, and he felt an ease flow through

him, the melting of joy. He floated. His visceral extension
arising from the water like a periscope. Gratitude abounding.
Wonder, astonishment, at how the simple joy of being alive
could fill him, melt, flow out into the water, then fill him up
again. Gazing up at her shadowed face, backlit by the amazing
rays of the firmament, he wept more openly.

"Are you *crying*?" she said.

"Maybe," he said. "Don't let go." Fast in her sure grip,
her steady hands, rolling over into a dead man's float was
utterly out of the question.

"Hey!"

It was not Cathy. Cathy had not altered her voice to a
deeper, meaner tone and shouted *hey*. It came from behind
and above her. From a woman standing at the verge of the
pool. Cathy seemed to waver, to swoon. Then to puke. It
started as a hiccup, one of Arlon's hiccups, from which puke
cascaded with each successive hiccup, up from her belly
and throat, out of her mouth, onto his belly—hot vomit
like maple syrup!—and into the water of the pool. Through
it all, her hands never wavered, one beneath him, one
clinging lovingly to his periscope.

"Hey! What do you think you're doing?"

She would not let them be. All the joy in the world could
melt.

"I'm calling the cops!"

Disengaging. Liquid slaps and splashes. He climbed
from the pool. Cathy grasped the verge, steadying herself.
He stood facing the strange, mean woman with blue pants
and a knapsack, his erection pointing rudely. Glancing
down, the mean woman recoiled. "What's the matter,
lady?" he slurred. "Never seen a belly button before?"

For the next five or six weekends, they met on Friday night
at their Holiday Inn just south of Harmony Mills to drink,

eat, laugh and make love. They discovered new restaurants, avoiding the bar downstairs, the pool and the woman in blue pants. They both confessed they didn't own a swimming suit anyhow. A little place called Scott's Tavern became a favorite, where the beer was ice cold, the gin and tonics tall, frosty and garnished with plump wedges of lime, the steaks tender and tasty. On Saturday afternoons they took long rides exploring the countryside, or shopping, or, on two rainy occasions, remaining in bed with a bottle of wine. Bottles of wine. The first weekend together they missed was in August, when Cathy had to help her daughter, Ellen, move back to college.

The next weekend was particularly festive, as if they'd been apart months, not days, and it was on that weekend, at Scott's Tavern drinking gin gimlets before dinner, that Cathy first used the "L" word. He didn't shy away, didn't recoil, when she told him she loved him, nor did he reciprocate. He pretended to take it for granted, pretended it was nothing out of the ordinary, just another little load in a life full of burdens. Later when she said it again, he hushed her with a finger to her lips. "Shh," he said. "Don't jinx it."

Then summer was gone. They missed most of September when his job took him to Michigan. He was auditing a GM dealership in Butler, which required an extended stay at corporate headquarters. She called him nearly every day and they talked about whatever was on their minds, the weather, their families, Final Jeopardy, what they'd had to eat, how many drinks they'd had, and of what, the latter with some specificity. Her mother knew she'd fallen off the wagon, she told him. Cathy had never confessed it, never discussed it, but her mother knew; she'd always had the power to divine what Cathy was thinking, or doing, almost before Cathy herself knew. This particular maternal phenomenon apparently had skipped a generation: the private life of her own daughter, Ellen, was mostly a mystery to Cathy. He was not surprised. Cathy was far too immersed in her own life to be much concerned with how others were living theirs. He told her his own kids, both away at college, had no idea their father was not happily rehabilitated, that he was not totally and happily dry. It was his duty to keep them deluded.

It grew to be routine. During the weeks they talked on the phone, she began to become someone he used to know.

In early October they met again at their Holiday Inn. The pool was closed, darkness falling early. They made love satisfyingly enough, had a good bottle of wine with their steaks at Scott's Tavern, and Cathy chattered on ebulliently, seemingly drunker than she should have been, seemingly oblivious to the fact that he had not much to say.

Then, just before Thanksgiving, her father died. Although he was seventy-five, it was nevertheless unexpected, and when she told him about it on the phone it was apparent she was on brittle ground. She dismissed Andrew almost as an afterthought, said she would be in touch, declining his offer to come to Hartsgrove; it was not a good time for him to meet her mother. He felt a bit diminished, a bit taken aback that his stature in her life had apparently been overshadowed all along by that of another man, her father, a man whom she'd mentioned only infrequently—albeit, he realized in hindsight, with something like awe.

His son was a freshman, his daughter a junior, and they both came home for Thanksgiving. He was not about to attempt a turkey, being loathe at any rate to celebrate at his home, to pull out the good china and silverware and perform a parody of the Thanksgivings they'd celebrated there, with Gretchen, for so many years. Too civilized. It occurred to him that much of his trouble was due to his being too civilized. Had he misled Gretchen? Because of his craggy good looks, his flannel shirts, because his father and his big brother had both been outdoorsmen, lettermen, stars, had she believed that he was that sort of man as well? The sort of man to punch and pummel the fellow with the stubble he caught kissing and pawing his drunken, willing wife at the Rathskellar that New Year's Eve so many years ago? Instead of gently leading her home and forgiving her—forgiving her before she asked for forgiveness, something she never got around to doing.

He took his kids to a restaurant that Thanksgiving. He ordered the trout.

A couple of weeks before Christmas, Cathy called. Could they meet Friday? She wanted to see him. She needed to see him.

Of course, he said. "Are you all right?"

"As good as can be expected, I guess."

"I guess it was quite a shock." He stared at the shadows in the empty corner of his living room where a tree should be standing by now.

"It keeps happening," she said.

"It does? What does?"

"Men," she said, "men I love. He was only seventy-five."

He felt a chill, glancing toward the drawer in the desk where he'd stashed his brand new .22 pistol, like a buried accusation. "You sure you're all right?" he said.

"Seventy-five is *not* that old." She sounded angry.

"Tell you what, why don't you come down here? The kids'll be home, I'd like them to meet you. It's about time you met them." She agreed. Hanging up, he sat back, looking away from the desk drawer to the shadowed, empty, Christmas tree corner. He took a deep breath, turning up the three-way lamp to bright. Grabbing his jacket, he headed out to buy a tree.

◆   ◆   ◆

Both the kids begged off. His daughter accepted a last-minute invitation to go skiing with her boyfriend's family, and his son had to stick around for a banquet at the convention hall where he'd taken a part-time job. They'd both be home next week, they assured him, and they'd meet his lady friend another day. He was proud of them both, of their independence, their confidence. They'd survived Gretchen's treachery, had clawed their way above it, and had grown, seemingly overnight, into adults, green versions perhaps, but adults nonetheless, out in the world on their own. Hanging up, he sat back, looking away from the desk drawer to the shadowed corner where leaned the scraggly Christmas tree, still captive in its plastic constraints. He'd never even gotten it into water, much less pulled the decorations down from the attic.

Despite her GPS, Cathy got lost trying to find her way to his house in Tarentum. It took three calls before he'd successfully guided her to him. She seemed to be drunk when she got there, flushed, red-eyed, though uncommonly solemn. He took her to Jason's Beanery, which, despite its name, was one of the town's premier restaurants, a stodgy old establishment where the waiters wore black vests and bowties over shirts as white and starched as the tablecloths. He and Gretchen had celebrated a couple of anniversaries there, years ago.

High tin ceilings, candlelight, crisp white linens, Christmas trees festive with tiny white lights, like distant stars, an elegant ambiance. In the soft light, Cathy's eyes looked even more ravished, as if she'd cried for days and couldn't conceal the evidence. When the maître d' had seated them at a spacious round table in the corner, the waiter appeared instantly, greeting them with the second grand flourish with which they'd been greeted in a matter of minutes. Could he bring them something to drink?

"Is a wild bear Catholic?" said Andrew, and the waiter lifted an eyebrow.

He ordered a bottle of Dom Perignon, and when Cathy whispered did he realize it was three hundred and twenty-five dollars a bottle, he called the waiter back, said make that two. They were celebrating. And they were celebrating not only for the two of them, he pointed out, but for seven. At least seven. Was he counting right? They had to celebrate for her father, of course, who was beyond earthly celebration, and they had to celebrate for the other dearly departed, or, at the very least, the dearly absent, those who were unable to join them for this celebration—his daughter, for instance, and his son, not to mention Cathy's daughter and mother, and even, in the magnanimous, forgiving spirit of the season, for the mother of his children, Wretched Gretchen. Cathy, willing to play along until that moment, frowned at the mention of the name, as if trying to remember all that it meant. A choir sang "Deck the Halls" in the background, *fa la la la la, la la, la la*, and he said, see? What did I just tell you? and sang along, just loud enough to almost embarrass her. "Aren't you in a mood," she said.

He looked at her with his silliest smirk. "Aren't I?" he said. "Aren't I indeed? Aren't you? In a mood? Great word, mood—moood, moooood, moooooooood."

"Sorry I asked, Bessie," she said.

After deciding that prime rib and Yorkshire pudding were a fine, traditional Christmas meal, and asking if they had it medium rare, and asking if they had an end cut, and being assured by the waiter that they had both, but that, of course, the two were mutually exclusive, Andrew said great, I'll have the lobster. By the time dessert arrived—Bananas Foster, Crème Brûlée—they'd finished both bottles of Dom Perignon. He ordered another.

When they finally left, the air outside was alive, dancing with snow flurries, and Cathy caught up to his silliness, her immunity having been compromised by copious doses of Dom Perignon. "Perfect!" she said. Giggling like a little girl, she caught a few flakes on her tongue on the way to the car, and, when he warned her to be watchful for night pigeons dropping surprises, she shoved him.

He wanted to go to the playground. He felt like a kid again, it was Christmas, it was snowing. She warmed to the idea immediately. It was where he used to take his kids to play, not far from his house, an elementary school playground, where a streetlight in the corner of the parking lot cast a glow that sparkled off the snowflakes floating down, and they played, chasing around horsies and cars, see-saws and slides. He pushed her on the swing, then went on himself, seeing how high he could go before bailing out into the black night air, shouting *Geronimo!* like he did when he was kid, showing off as he used to then, though landing much more harshly. Much less joyfully. If there was a single moment when it turned, that was it: when he landed, in the dark, roughly, without joy, when he realized that the joy was gone for good. They began to feel the cold, and got into his car, but he didn't start it. He didn't want it to end, he said, without a lot of sincerity. He felt so limp, so suddenly. They caught their breath, breathed. Cathy grew impatient. She began to kiss him, lick and touch and fondle, thinking to prompt him into taking her home, but when he didn't, sitting impassively, she unzipped his trousers, and despite his obvious arousal, he still barely moved, and she couldn't wait. He watched, listening to the sounds of wetness and breathing, the moaning of the woman so earnestly at her work. When she was finished, he was finished. She took a deep breath, her head still on his lap, and he listened, waiting for her to exhale, but she never did. Never that he heard. She might have been asleep. And it was Gretchen's head on his lap. And he imagined it on the laps of strangers. Wretched Gretchen.

4. Ellen

They sat in a back pew, alone, in the big church with the vaulted dome, light streaming in, a dozen alabaster cherubs watching over them from above. The words of the priest were artificially magnified, unnaturally intimate, uttered as they were into a microphone hidden in his vestments. Andrew McAninch had loving children, he said, and Ellen spotted them—at least the two most likely candidates—in the front pew near the coffin that was covered with a pall of crisp, white linen. A red-headed girl and a boy with a buzz cut. When she could crane her neck no longer, Ellen stood, taller than she wished, and scanned the congregation, the back of every head, up one row and down the next, withstanding the glances of the priest.

"I told you she wouldn't be here," Glory whispered when Ellen sat back down. "Funerals are not your mother's thing."

Funerals were not Ellen's thing either—exactly whose thing were they?—and she remembered the last one, scarcely a month before, in a smaller, darker church, sitting beside her mother as they praised her grandfather, before putting him into the ground. The red-headed girl at the front of the church—she should be feeling the same things her mother had felt that day, staring at the coffin of her father, the same things Ellen never got to feel at her own father's funeral. She'd been only two. She wouldn't know how to feel when they bury your father. What should you feel? Anything more than at any other funeral? *Dread* would sum it up best. Dragging your own funeral around inside you, every day, day after day, like those extra pounds you've been meaning to lose. She had years, however. She took her grandmother's hand, bony and dry, and she squeezed it, and Glory squeezed back, and from the corner of her eye she saw Glory's delicate, firm jaw, the slight tremble there. The tremble of the condemned.

Contempt. It dawned on Ellen that contempt best summed up Glory; it was a pillar of her personality. Now she was struggling to hold death in as much contempt as she'd always held most things in life, and the futility of the struggle was showing. Ellen felt—to her shame, to her utter satisfaction—a sense of triumph in Glory's futility.

After the funeral they went to the house. The address had been announced after the service, but Ellen didn't need it; she'd already entered it into her grandmother's GPS early that morning. It occurred to her that the invitation, open and general as it was, did specify family and friends, and they could by no means qualify as either; she wondered if that might trouble her reluctant companion. After she'd parked the BMW at the end of the long line of cars, she mentioned it, hoping it might. They were walking toward McAninch's, five houses down on the quiet suburban street of trees and shrubs and older ranch houses. In the front yard by the curb lay a slush-covered Christmas tree, never used, still bound in plastic mesh. Glory said, "Your mother was, by all indications, a friend of his. I should think that would make us friends by proxy."

"Long-lost," Ellen said, looking down at her grandmother.

There'd been music after her grandfather's funeral, noise in the house, conversations both loud and soft, containing much remembrance and sadness to be sure, but the occasional spike of laughter as well, thanks in large part to Cathy. The McAninch home was quiet and somber. Faces stared at them upon their arrival; after that, they might have been invisible. Through the people they made their way to the kitchen. There, standing by the french doors that led out to a wooden deck, stood the red-headed girl, in a circle of four or five other, older people, a red-headed woman among them. The boy with the buzz-cut, the one Ellen took to be the son, stood near them, not with them, looking out through the door at the snow melting on the deck. Ellen reached for a muffin on the bountiful countertop. Glory slapped her hand lightly. Ellen took the muffin anyway, took a bite, feeling fat and sad. Glory, barging in undaunted, introduced them to the circle of relatives.

"You're related to Cathy Northey?" said the red-headed girl.

"She's my daughter," Glory said.

"She's my mother," said Ellen, swallowing muffin.

"Where is *she?*" the girl wanted to know. Despite her face that was pretty and placid, her sharp green eyes showed alarm. "*She's* the one we want to see."

Ellen saw revulsion in their eyes as well, fear, as they beheld her and her mother.

"Actually," said Ellen, "we're looking for her too. We thought she might be here."

Glory said, "Did he, Andrew, say anything before . . . Did he know her well?"

"Yes," said the red-headed girl. "He was concerned about her. He wanted us to meet her—he was concerned because her father had just died, he said she was very upset by it. He was to meet her here that night, the night . . ."

"He was with a woman," said the red-headed lady, the older one. Ellen thought she must be the girl's mother, the estranged wife of Andrew McAninch. "He was seen in a restaurant with some woman that nobody knows. It must have been her."

"He met her in rehab," the girl said. "He was supposedly dry."

"Yet when they found him," the older woman said, "he had enough booze in him to float a battleship."

"A *destroyer*," said the boy, who'd joined the circle. Ellen was surprised he spoke at all, so glazed were his eyes. Pimples on his forehead up into his hair. "Enough to float a destroyer."

"So no one knows," said Glory. The tremble was gone from her chin, the contempt back in command. "No one knows where my daughter is."

The red-headed lady raised her own chin. "No. And the police are looking for her too."

"The police?" Ellen said.

"Why?" Glory said. "Wasn't it a simple—perhaps I should say straightforward—matter of suicide?"

"Perhaps," said the red-headed lady, a blaze flaring in her eyes. "But I, for one, can't help but wonder how the gun ended up in the backseat."

"Please," said the girl, with wet gleaming eyes. "Please. We want to know what she knows, we have to know what happened. Where *is* she?"

"There were fingerprints on the gun," said an old man standing there. "Besides his."

"Beside his, too," said the boy with the buzz-cut, his eyes turning inward. "Besides his, beside his. He was probably beside himself."

"Hurry," Glory said as they walked down the sidewalk away from the McAninch house. Ellen didn't have to be told. Nothing more was said until they were out of Tarentum, until Ellen asked where they were going. "To your grandfather's camp," Glory said.

The red-headed girl's words came back to Ellen then, too, how very concerned Andrew had been about Cathy, how very hard she was taking her father's death. "Your mother was so crazy about him," Glory said. "She worshipped him." Of course she did. It should have been the first place they looked.

The road followed the river, meandering through forest. Apprehension overcame Ellen, leaving its damp palm-prints on the steering wheel. For the first time in years the memory returned, one of her earliest, of her and her mother playing hide and seek—for that was what Cathy had told her they were doing at the time—the sweaty palms and held breath, the racing heart, her mother holding her so close she could feel her mother's heartbeat as well, Malachy Mouse tucked safely between them as they hid in the closet from the footsteps tromping all through the house, shadows passing in front of the crack of light at the door. Ellen would not learn until many years later, and then only by accident, that it had been the authorities seeking them, Family Court officials they were hiding from: her grandmother, Glory, was seeking to wrest custody of her granddaughter from her daughter.

Just beyond a bend, in the river and in the road, a smaller, unpaved road, twin tracks, headed through the trees. There wasn't much snow. Tires crunching. It was entirely passable. The camp was in an opening where the river was wide, a small building, shabby white clapboards and a tin roof nearly the same color as the ice-covered river. And Cathy's car.

Ellen pulled her grandmother's BMW behind the red Volkswagen bug, and they sat watching the camp. There was no sign of life.

Anywhere. No birds in the air, no movement on the river, no breeze to stir the tops of the trees. No life anywhere, only them and their breathing.

"You wait here," Glory said. "I'll go in."

Ellen didn't move.

She watched Glory walk across the snow, moving gingerly, looking all of her seventy-three years. She watched her go into the building.

She waited. She watched the still-life of the river and the trees, and found herself holding her breath. No signs of life.

Then she got out, following her grandmother's footsteps.

Cathy was on the plain little couch in the front room. She'd wrapped herself in an old, dusty-smelling comforter. The empty bottle of pills on the table by her head had a faded label, a prescription dated years ago. When Ellen realized she'd seen it before, often, for as long as she could remember, in her mother's purse whenever Cathy had fumbled for her keys or her lipstick, her knees buckled. She felt dizzy, too tall, towering over her grandmother standing there looking down at her mother. Only her mother's face was visible above the comforter, her face and her messy, straw-colored hair like a bird's nest, and Ellen, seeing her mother in the dim light—for Glory, standing motionless, expressionless, had not switched on the lamp—was surprised at the amount of anger polluting her sorrow.

The note seemed to have been an afterthought, scribbled in a shaky hand, perhaps after the pills had begun to take effect. All it said was that she was sorry, she loved them, please forgive her. It made no mention of Andrew.

Ellen saw something else then, beside her mother's cheek poking up from under the old comforter, a frayed little wisp of a tail. She pulled back the cover, saw Malachy Mouse clutched to her mother's breast.

"That damned thing," said Glory.

TILLIE DINGER

1953

From miles around they came to bear witness. What they witnessed were six men, three sheriff's deputies, the coroner and two of his assistants, striding across the furrows of Lester Fiscus' seven acre field, over the hillock in the middle, down to the tree line below and back again in a pattern laid out by the sheriff for the purpose of covering every square inch of the field. Each man carried a bag, and each man stopped every so often to bend and pluck an object from the earth with his gloved hand, and drop it into the bag. Their harvest was bones, human bones. Each man also wore his handkerchief over his face, to ward off the stench of the freshly fertilized field, an offensive odor stronger than any they could recall, and no man there was a stranger to fertilized fields. Some of the witnesses, the nearly two dozen men, women and children who'd gathered to watch in somber silence, wore similar coverings over their faces, many fanning the air before their noses, trying to banish the malodorous air. On the upper corner of the field, toward where the weather-beaten barn and house sat in sullen disrepair, Sheriff Foulkrod stood at a wary distance beside Lester Fiscus, both men in a wary stance, feet planted solidly in the soil, arms crossed over their chests, service revolver protruding at Foulkrod's hip. Neither man's face was covered. Tillie Craven, one of the watchers, was not surprised that neither man would hide behind a hankie, thereby showing weakness. She noticed how handsome Lester Fiscus was, at least at a distance far enough to remove from consideration his oft-broken nose, teeth and scowl.

The sheriff, it was generally acknowledged, had it in for Lester Fiscus. He'd been driving by Fiscus' isolated farm in his cruiser the day before—a near daily part of his patrol, keeping tabs on Fiscus—when he'd noticed peculiar white objects glinting in the low sun across the field, and had stopped for a closer look. It soon became apparent the objects were pieces of bone, and the sheriff had persisted, hoping against hope, finally hitting the jackpot: a piece that looked for all the world to belong to the eye socket of a human skull. Word had quickly spread.

Tillie Craven had more than a passing interest in the bones, but less of an interest, it occurred to her as she looked down the road at the other spectators, than the McCrackens, whom she spotted off to themselves close to where the sheriff stood near Lester Fiscus. Luke McCracken put his arm around his wife, Ethel, but she shrugged it off, staring intently at the men harvesting the bones. It was a chilly October afternoon beneath a sky so plain and gray it promised nothing. Just over three years before, the McCrackens' two youngest daughters, Mary Lou and Katie, had wandered into the woods and vanished. Luke and Ethel were wondering, Tillie reckoned, just how big were the bones being plucked from the field.

Tillie made her way over to offer what comfort she could. She was a small woman, built like a twig, and the McCrackens never saw her coming till she was there. "How you folks doing?" she said. Luke and Ethel nodded in unison, regarding her as they might somebody's nosing dog. Luke asked her who was minding the store, though they all knew it would be Chester, Tillie's husband, proprietor and owner of the Coolbrook General Store, who always minded it when Tillie was out gallivanting about.

"Hey, Sheriff," called Tillie, offering comfort, "how big are them bones?"

An audible gasp from the McCrackens, as watchers up and down the road turned toward Tillie, a tide of shaking faces.

"I know," called the sheriff. "I know, Tillie."

Everybody knew Tillie. Before she married Chester Craven she was Tillie Dinger, the preacher's daughter, a high-spirited, immodest girl, too high-spirited and immodest in the minds of many. Her reputation was made at the age of eleven some thirty-five years before, when she'd been exposed as the miscreant who'd poked out the knothole in a plank behind the boys' outhouse and charged the other fourth and fifth grade girls of Coolbrook Township School a penny a peek to see what the boys peed with. Unfortunately, the knothole being near the bottom of the plank, Ron Fenstemaker had heard the giggles, spotted the source, and peed in Mary Lou Lemon's eye. Tillie's father, the preacher at Coolbrook Baptist Church, had endured the ensuing scandals, all those that followed, aware that the good Lord was testing his faith, much as He'd tested Job's. Tillie's knees to this day were calloused and calcified from hours of enforced prayer on the hard plank floor of her room.

Chester had always been there. The Coolbrook General Store was only a few doors down the road—literally down, as the village was on the side of a hill—from the house near the church where Tillie lived, and Chester had a place in her earliest memories, helping his parents at the store whenever Tillie came in with her mother for a loaf of bread, or by herself for penny candy, on the days when she'd managed to liberate a penny from her father's pocket. To this day, the squeaking of a screen door opening, the slap of it slamming shut, reminded her of the store's big front door in summer, the sweating of an icy pop bottle, the saltiness of sweaty skin, and the eyes of Chester following her around the store. His eyes were big and gray behind his spectacles, and they always seemed to be on her, and not, he would assure her later, to see what she might be stealing. It was because, he was to confess, he simply couldn't keep his eyes off her. Even after the influenza had taken both his parents and he found himself proprietor of the steady little store on his own at the age of eighteen, even then, at his most tried and harried, he'd always had eyes for Tillie. And it was that, maybe—for Tillie never really understood the reason— because he was the only man who ever purely adored her, who ever heaped his attention upon her for any benign reason, the man who was always there like the sun in the morning, maybe that was the reason she'd married him. For they had precious little else in common. And, after Chester's first heart attack, precious little less.

It was Tillie then who was left to heft the big bags of feed and flour, for, despite her diminutive size, she was strong and wiry, and it was Tillie who was left to climb the ladder to clean and stock the high shelves, for, against all expectations, she waged an obsessive war with soap and water against any and all manner of filth. And it was Tillie who was left to her own devices when it came to needs of a physical nature. The days of her being his little *Tilliedinger* faded away. The days of her whispering in his ear, *I got a Craven*, with a lick to his lobe and a free-roaming fondle, were gone as well.

Lester Fiscus would not be not the first. Chester's heart attack notwithstanding, Lester Fiscus still was not the first.

The bones were not those of the McCracken girls. The coroner, a gassy old man by the name of Snyder, pieced the puzzle back together the best he could and came up with an adult male, albeit an adult male with lots of pieces still missing. Tillie suspected as much. She suspected too that after three years, the news would be cold comfort to Luke and Ethel, for Luke and Ethel wanted to know where their missing daughters were, wanted to bury them and put them to rest, and the fact that their deaths had not yet been confirmed would serve only to prolong the agony. Tillie suspected as well that there was, nevertheless, a link between the girls and the bones in the field, although she suspected that revelation too would be of little comfort to the McCrackens.

What did Lester Fiscus know about the bones?

What did Tillie know about Lester Fiscus?

He stopped at the general store infrequently, and he always seemed, in Tillie's eye, to be drunk, a certain glassiness to his glowering eyes, a certain easy slur to the few words he ever uttered. Tillie was not offended. What did offend her though was his habit of only pricing items in the store, never buying. The axe. She remembered the fine Swedish axe, the way the blade of it glinted the same as Lester's eye when he touched it with the tips of his gnarly, dirty fingers. But he wasn't buying.

There was also the Dewdrop Inn on Weedville Road where Tillie often went to dance to Hank Williams songs on the juke box (without Chester, whose dancing days were done), but she'd seen Lester Fiscus there only once or twice, and she couldn't remember the last time. She didn't want to wait for another chance meeting.

When she drove by his place next day, the field was muddy and trampled, and his battered old pickup was in front of his house. By the door to the barn sat his Ford tractor, his Wain-Roy backhoe attached. Many a local farmer hired him, distasteful though most of them found it, to remove a stump, dig a ditch, excavate for a foundation. She wondered what else the backhoe might be good for. She suspected she knew. Finding nobody home, she wasn't surprised. She'd heard the sheriff had brought Lester in for questioning by the state police in an effort to solve the mystery of the bones, and seldom were those interrogations less than a day or two in length.

Next day it was raining and he came to the door when she pounded upon it, her Hudson steaming in the yard.

"What can I do for you, Tillie?"

"You can tell me where them bones came from."

"I'll tell you same as what I told the coppers—I ain't got no idea."

"I ain't buying that," she said.

Rain battered the tin roof of the porch. A cow's low from the barn sounded like a moan. Lester was none too clean, oily patches on his overalls, a faint whiff of manure. But he was solid, his stance suggesting hard muscle. He set his square, unshaven jaw and his glassy eyes underwent a shift, faltering from her face down the front of her dress, the moment Tillie was waiting to see. She didn't have an extra ounce on her, but the ounces she did have were right where they were supposed to be. "You got a bathtub in this place?" she asked Lester Fiscus.

Not far from Craven's store, at the top of the hill where the village ended and the road to Hartsgrove rounded a bend and leveled out, sat the Coolbrook Township School, a squat, green-shingled box of a building with a broad face of mullioned windows, and a sign, *Coolbrook Twp,* in large letters over the wide front doors. For over sixty years the place had been the hub of the lives of the youth of the township, and this was the first year those youths were able to avail themselves of indoor plumbing. After it had been installed in the late spring, the outhouses, scene of Tillie's first great dare, had been demolished, the holes filled in. When Tillie drove by, it was dark, still drizzling, and she couldn't make out the site beyond the rise in the middle of the schoolyard where the outhouses once had stood.

It was after closing, faint light coming from the store windows, scarcely enough to cast a shadow across the porch. The porch light was off, though the front door was still unlocked, a low jangle of bells when she opened it. Inside, she stood for a moment, taking in the dim interior, the worn and scarred countertop and the ancient cash register, the sly glinting of goods and stores stacked to the tin ceiling, the soft clicking of the clock, the quiet hum of the Coca-Cola cooler. Looking up, she thought she detected a speck of blood, but realized it was too dark, the ceiling all but invisible. It had to be her imagination, because of the bones. She found Chester in the back storeroom, asleep in the little chair among the crowded shelves, his head resting against one of the bolts of cotton fabric standing upright against the wall, the bolt of blue cloth with dark butterflies imprinted. Tillie had removed it from display three years before, after she'd sold the last yard to Ethel McCracken to make sundresses for her girls. Mary Lou McCracken, according to her family, had been wearing that very sundress when she'd vanished. How Chester had aged since his heart attack, turning paunchy and pasty, his hair turning thinner and whiter. A gleam of saliva leaked from his lips, his glasses askew on his face. He didn't stir when Tillie came near. She touched his cheek with the back of her hand, the fragile warmth. Chester woke, a cloud of confusion vacating his gray eyes as Tillie's face came into focus.

"What are you sleeping here for? Why ain't you up in bed?"

"I was trying to redd up some back here. Just set down a minute to rest."

"You oughtn't to be overdoing it, Chester. You know that."

"Redding up ain't exactly chopping wood. I gotta still be able to do something."

"I don't want nothing to happen to you."

Chester stood, stiffly, steadying himself with a hand to a shelf by a stack of canned peaches. He put an arm around Tillie, pulling her close. "Where you been?"

"Over and had a talk with Lester Fiscus," she said. "Wondering about them bones."

He released her, making his way toward the stairs. "What about the bones?"

"You heard they weren't the McCracken girls, didn't you?"

"Yep." He started up, slowly. "Those girls'll never be seen again. Why do you care so much about the bones?"

"Don't you care? Ain't you curious?" She hesitated at the bottom, watching him go up step by step, a rising sack of flour.

The sack of flour shrugged. He turned, gripping the handrail, looking down at Tillie still on the bottom. "A little bit, I suppose."

"Sheriff thinks the bones might belong to Marlin Fiscus." She started up behind him.

"Marlin Fiscus? Lester's brother?"

"That's what the sheriff's saying." Or so Lester Fiscus

had told her. At one time she'd known Marlin Fiscus better than Lester, as Marlin was older, closer to Tillie's age, and she remembered him from their school days, though she hadn't seen much of him since. No one had. Tillie, and, she suspected, about everyone else, had taken Lester at his word when he'd said that Marlin had left in a huff, headed out west to find his fortune there, after their father had left the farm to Lester. The sheriff, it turned out, had his doubts, suspicions caused foremost by Lester's penchant for solving disputes with his fists, or other violent means, as evidenced by the many complaints sworn against him by this neighbor and that, this bar patron and that. Then there was the matter of Lester's total disregard of the law, of authority in general, at least as far as the sheriff was concerned, having arrested him more than once for poaching deer, moonshining whiskey, availing himself of this item or that without benefit of proper payment. The sheriff even insinuated, or so Lester had told Tillie, that the circumstances surrounding the passing of old George Fiscus, the father, hadn't been all that clear-cut either.

It did little to satisfy Tillie's curiosity. She didn't want to know what the sheriff suspected, she wanted to know what Lester Fiscus knew. She wanted to know if indeed the bones were those of Marlin, if indeed Lester Fiscus was a man who could murder, for Tillie was intrigued by the possibility of that capability in any other living creature. She wanted to know everything there was to know about Lester Fiscus. That would require more work.

Chester sagged into the bed. Tillie lay down beside him. "He's no good," he said.

"Who?" She nestled close to her husband. "Lester Fiscus?"

"Lester Fiscus. An ornery, dangerous man. God knows what he's done, or could do."

"Oh, I know. Poor Lester." Then she said, "Do you happen to recollect who they got to tear down the outhouses up at the school?"

Chester scratched his chin, took off his glasses and looked at her. "I'd give a month's worth of gumballs," he said, "to know what's going on in that Mexican jumping bean mind of yours."

Gumballs and jumping beans hit her square on the funny bone and she laughed, the full-throated, belly-bouncing Tilliedinger laugh, which always triggered the same response in him, and he laughed too, the pair of them laughing toward the ceiling of the dark little bedroom, rolling and slapping the sheets, and squeezing each other's hands, until Chester had to stop, his laughter gone to coughing, his skin to ashen gray.

Two nights later the spotlight from Lester's pickup thrust a solid beam of pristine white light into the black of the woods, Tillie imagining it to be the saber of the Lord probing the blackness of her soul. The beam alighted on a bewildered doe, which froze in all its innocence. Lester aimed his thirty-ought-six, violence ensued, a spurt of black blood, and the doe crumbled to the forest floor. Lester let out a whoop. Tillie watched him trot across the field toward the spot at the edge of the woods where the doe had dropped, the woods that were vast and deep, the shadows of which seemed to be reaching out to seize Lester and swallow him whole. She saw her heartbeat quivering down the beam of light. He returned, dragging the doe, his skin white as bones in the light. She knelt beside him, beside the doe, in the dirt by the road, and when he slit open the belly of the animal with his knfe, she saw, clear as day, the puff of white vapor rushing out.

"You see that?" she said. "The ghost of the thing—why, it flew straight up."

"What?" he said. "The steam? The guts is hot, that's all." She wasn't convinced. She shook her head. "You're a preacher's kid all right," he said. He left the guts in a heap by the side of the road, threw the carcass in the bed of the truck. "Let's get on out of here," he said, "before the law shows up."

Tillie was thrilled. They set out on the isolated dirt road through the endless forest north of Hartsgrove, and when she noticed the glow of light behind them, probably the headlights of another car or truck, quite possibly, in Lester's mind, the headlights of the law, he gunned his Ford. They tore furiously down the road, Tillie jouncing wildly, nearly bumping her head on the ceiling of the cab, and looking back she saw the light still there, brighter if anything over the carcass bouncing in back, and Lester went even faster. Reaching down, he turned off his headlights. At first she couldn't see a thing, racing headlong into blackness, trying to tame the panic bucking inside her, expecting at any moment to burst through to oblivion, until finally, somehow, the road, the ditches, the woods began to ease out of the night, scarcely more than a suggestion, an idea, and Lester sped on, unperturbed, bouncing blindly, off the dirt road onto a trail, little more than a logging trail, then onto a path, then onto nothing. The lights behind them were long lost. They might have been lost as well, in the heart of the forest, a woods so vast and trackless that Tillie felt less than a speck of dirt, a tiny, pulsing speck of dirt.

In the bed of the truck her blood kept racing even as the pickup was still and steaming and ticking, its heart still racing as well, the woods watching, listening. Lester's animal grunts, the squeals of other creatures. The smell of the doe's blood was like the scent of clover in the spring, the dead flesh still warm, a source of comfort against the chill night air.

♦   ♦   ♦

How Tillie went about her business: She got Lester Fiscus in a delicate position, a position in which, in her experience, men were prone to tell the truth, because, in that position, men's thoughts were focused such that the creation of a lie was beyond their capability at the time. He told her he didn't know where the bones had come from. He told her he didn't stand guard over his manure pile and that anyone might have come by when he was out in his fields driving his clattering, rackety tractor and could have put anything they wanted in that pile. A good way to dispose of a body. Or, for all he knew, some hobo could have fallen asleep trying to keep warm and sunk to the bottom and rotted there for a year or two—he hadn't done much fertilizing for a while, not until this fall—and yes, the beaters on his manure spreader had seemed a little bulky and clunky, but he'd thought it was just from rust and neglect and disuse, not from the shredding of bones. He knew nothing about the origin of the bones, he professed, and Tillie came around to believing him. Then she let him finish.

When Tillie stepped out of the store to greet Shingledecker's Bakery truck, the early afternoon sun had broken through and she looked up to see the white clouds flocking like sheep in a blue pasture, thinking of God the shepherd, as she often did. Everywhere, dead leaves were dropping from trees. Old man Radaker was driving by in his battered Chevy pickup, up the hill toward the church, which put her in mind of the time she and Martha Long decided to break Tillie's dog, Luther, of chasing cars. They'd been led to believe that throwing a bucketful of water on the offending pup was good for that purpose, and so they'd had Martha's daddy drive them by in the bed of his pickup, and when Luther commenced chasing, Tillie was to throw the water on him, not accounting for the bump and the lurch that caused her to fling the water on Martha instead. Funny at the time, or so Tillie had believed, gales of laughter in the wind, though looking back, much of the humor was lost after Martha had not spoken to her in any meaningful way since then. Tillie didn't have many female friends.

Back inside the store, she caught Chester up on the ladder, stacking cans of Spam. "Get down from there, mister," she said. "You *trying* to kill yourself?"

"Jesus, Tillie, just let me be." He looked down, too gray for her liking, too damp and clammy, his glasses fogging. "I gotta mind the store."

"That's why you got me here, Chester."

"You ain't always here. Lots of times you ain't here."

"Well, cans of Spam can wait till I am." She didn't account for the rhyme until she saw the look on Chester's face staring down, his cheeks starting to lift his glasses, the chuckle already working its way up from his belly, and they both laughed, a bit too hard, the laughter of one feeding off the other as it always did. He clung to the ladder, Tillie taking him by the knee and hugging, then tugging, coaxing him down.

When he started coughing, she led him by the hand to the rocker behind the counter. "You sit there. You wait for customers. You let me take care of everything else." She climbed the ladder to deal with the cans of Spam while he watched from his chair, his hanky in his hand to wipe his face. "Chester," she said, scolding, "this here shelf's filthy." He watched her, shook his head.

No one came in for a while. Early afternoons were generally slow. She got the cans down from the shelf, got herself a bucket of hot water, swished in her Spic and Span, then climbed back up to scrub the shelf. Chester's eyes had closed, the gentle rocking of the chair had quit, and he appeared to be napping. Time was, not that long ago, he never napped. Cleaning the shelves with soap and water, as she often did, always put her in mind of Curly Smathers, not a pleasant image by any means, so she scrubbed all the harder, trying to scrub that bald and vicious man out of her mind as well. The Smatherses, a mean, rough, dirty tribe, nasty hillbillies all, were about extinct now. She didn't know of another still walking the earth. Not long after Curly's last visitation, she'd heard that his old man, Vern, had been found dead in his bed, his throat cut, as near as they could tell. His body had been there for months, not much more than bones by the time he was discovered. It was the talk of the township. All this was right around the time the McCracken girls had vanished.

"Do you love him, Tillie?"

Chester's voice startled the brush right out of her hand, splashing with a clatter to the floor. Descending the ladder to fetch it, she looked over at him, his eyes still closed. "What are you talking about? Do I love who?"

Her husband's eyes remained shut, though the chair gave a gentle rock.

Truth was, the question baffled her. Tillie had always been in love; Tillie had never been in love. "You ain't talking about Lester Fiscus, are you? That's just plain dumb. You asking me if I'm in love with Lester Fiscus?" Chester didn't answer. The rocking chair quietly squawked. She said, "I told you I was just curious about them bones. I told you I was just getting acquainted with him to find out what he knows about them bones." She knew she was talking too much. She climbed the ladder, brush in hand, commenced her scrubbing again. "Besides, I only danced with him once or twice. A body's got to have somebody to dance with." The last was quieter, almost to herself.

Life will not hand you joy, Tillie knew that. Life will not

cut a big slice of happiness and hand it over to you and say, here, this is for you—go ahead, enjoy it. You had to go out and dig and search and scour and find it for yourself, happiness, and then you had to grab it with both hands and live it. She was afraid Chester didn't possess this knowledge. And even if he were to learn it now, it was probably too late.

She scrubbed hard. She worked up a good sweat. Chester's chair had stopped again. He appeared, again, to be napping. Annoyed, Tillie scrubbed till the splinters gave way. Not a customer came in to save her. She paused at the top of the ladder, her muscles tingling, glowing, and she looked around the store in the quiet. The Coca-Cola cooler hummed loudly—louder than usual—by the front window, the only sound but for the soft ticking of the clock, the windows bright with afternoon sun casting shadows through the store, glinting off the top of the cooler and the floorboards below. Goods in cans and stacks and heaps, baskets and barrels, food stuffs mostly, sustenance, life. She felt secure, fortunate, grateful, bored and restless.

Out of the quiet again came Chester's voice. "You ever had a broken heart, Tillie?"

She sighed. Once again she was unequipped to answer the question. "Yes," she said, and resumed her scrubbing. "When Luther—you remember Luther, my dog—got hit by that car. That purt near broke my heart."

Chester didn't open his eyes. He never stirred, not until Meryl Fenstemaker came in to buy a new broom for his wife, Betty, when the bells on the door gave a tired, happy jangle.

The Dewdrop Inn was cutting edge, the first building in the vicinity to find itself sheathed in wide swaths of aluminum. The white siding gave the place, a two-story, featureless affair, a sterile, tinny look alongside the well-traveled road. Inside, however, it was dark and plain as ever, a long, unembellished bar, a floor of worn and darkened boards, an eclectic collection of cheap tables and chairs that had been in place for years. Cluttering the walls, beer signs of every variety, some plugged in and glowing bright. Business had always been good. There weren't many watering holes along the twelve-mile stretch of road between Hartsgrove and Weedville, and the place served as an oasis in the wooded, rural countryside.

The juke box in a back corner was loud and garish with neon reds and blues. Lester Fiscus dropped in a nickel and played "Your Cheatin' Heart."

Tillie cocked her head and said, "You ain't funny, you know."

"Ain't I?" he said with a cocky grin.

"Shut up and dance," she said.

Lester was an awful dancer, but what he lacked in grace he made up for in confidence, holding her close, gripping her tight. His aversion to dancing did not deter Tillie in the least, as she loved to dance, and dancing was the price Lester would have to pay for admission. This evening, midweek, they had the dance floor to themselves, the only other patrons being five or six of the regulars, salesmen, mechanics, men with no jobs, all of whom Tillie knew by name. Behind the bar, Herschel Smith, the owner, kept a wary eye out. A burly man still, despite his age, he'd broken up more fights than he cared to recall over the years, more than one of which had featured Lester Fiscus.

When they weren't dancing, Tillie and Lester drank at the far end of the bar, alone. She drank rum and cokes, standing close, her hand on his knee as he hunkered on his bar stool with ten-cent shots of whiskey and Iron City drafts. "Let's get out of here," he said, looking up at the Rolling

Rock clock behind the bar. Morning chores came early, and his cows weren't prone to sleeping in. That was the excuse he used.

"I ain't done dancing yet," Tillie said.

He finished his beer, shoved the glass toward Hershey, wiped his mouth with the back of his hand. "So, what's your old man up to tonight?"

"What do you care what Chester's up to?" The Tilliedinger temper flared for an instant. "Mind your own damn business."

"I am," he said. "That's exactly what I'm doing."

She removed her hand, stepping away from his knee. "Who'd they get to tear down them outhouses up at the school last spring? Was it you? Did you have anything to do with that?"

Lester scratched his head. "Where the hell'd that come from?"

"I want to know is all. Tell me."

"What do you want to know for?"

"Was it you that tore 'em down, or wasn't it?"

The crooked Fiscus grin beneath the crooked nose. "How bad do you want to know?"

Tillie touched his cheek and ear, not too hard, not too soft, looking him in the eye where the lust was overflowing. She'd find out later. She knew how to find out later.

When Chester arrived, Tillie and Lester were dancing to "Vaya con Dios," sweaty and pawing and eager. Hershey, busy behind the bar, never looked up, nor did the two old men still lingering there, drunk and oblivious. Only Tillie saw the door open, saw Chester step quietly inside and pause in the doorway, his eyes immediately finding hers. The light from the lamppost in the parking lot fell across his shoulders and wispy white hair, and, to Tillie, it looked for all the world like a halo. It looked to her like the very coming of the Lord, and she stopped and trembled, her hands dropping, then she fell to her knees on the dance floor.

This confused Lester, Tillie falling from his embrace to kneel before him. He caught his breath, and looked around to see if maybe Hershey had stepped in back, if the others were gone and they were alone, and that was when he too saw Chester.

Chester came toward them.

Tillie began to cry. She watched through her tears, the tears refracting the lights from the juke box, and the glowing beer signs and the bulb above the pool table, and it was as though she were watching his approach through stained glass, through the hues of heaven and hell. Chester was not the Lord, of course, she knew that, but she knew, just as surely, that it was the Lord coming to her in Chester. The Lord was acting through her husband, who was His instrument. Her knees gripped the floor in her prayerful stance, and she clasped her hands before her chest, and began to chant and pray, "No, Chester, please Chester, no Chester, please . . ."

This confused Lester even more. Was Tillie afraid? Was she fearful of what Chester, this pudgy, lumpy, doughy soft man, might do to her? To *him*? A sneer of biblical proportions descended upon his face.

"Please, Chester, no, no, no, please. Please don't do it— please. I need you, Chester." Her pleading face looked up to her husband, this man, preparing to lay down his life, preparing to die for her sins. The halo had become a crown of thorns.

Chester touched her head, a benediction. Then he looked at Lester Fiscus, crossly, his spectacles catching a sharp spark of light.

"This is my wife."

Lester said, "Yeah, so what? I know that. So what?"

"This is the woman I love," Chester said.

More was said, but those were the last words Tillie recalled when she looked back on it over the years, over the decades. She remembered those words, followed by others, harsh, loud words in a jumbled torrent, then pushes and shoves, then fists, work boots thumping the floorboards about her in a manic, mad scrambling dance. Then Chester on his back on the dark, dirty floor, his hand reaching toward her, and the way his eyelids fluttered over his loving gaze.

1983

Tillie tiptoed down the hallway, slipped inside the room, eased the door shut behind her, and took off her clothes. The old man looked up from the bed where he was reading, his face a confusion of dread and delight.

"Jesus, Tillie, you don't waste no time, do you?"

"At our age, Sam, we ain't got no time to waste."

"Look at you," he said. And he did, over his glasses, his eyes filling up.

"Oh, I ain't much to look at anymore. Never was, I guess, but one good thing is I never had enough meat on me to sag when I got old."

"I used to have the body of a Greek god," Sam said. "Now I'm built like a goddamn Greek."

She climbed into his bed under the covers beside him and reached into his pajama bottoms, and Sam shivered and gave her a squeeze, and they laughed and were filled for an instant with happiness, though it was entirely uncertain at this point what, if anything, might ensue. How she liked Sam, he was one of her favorites, though his penchant for the odd outburst of tears whenever he thought of his dead wife, Alice, Tillie always found disconcerting. It could happen anytime, at bingo, at supper, it could happen when he was playing the bongos on the waste cans in their make-up band on Wednesday afternoons. Still, after all these years, she grieved for Chester every bit as much, but life had to be lived.

Down the hallway beyond the door, someone called her name. Brenda, the nurse.

"Damn," Tillie said.

"Shit," said Sam.

"Why can't they just leave me be?" she said, clutching Sam. Another voice called her name, Mrs. Carrier, mean Mrs. Carrier, the night shift supervisor. It was Brenda and Mrs. Carrier looking for her, and Sam and Tillie heard doors opening, questions being asked, irritated responses, and they were opening every door, coming closer to Sam's.

"Want to hide?" said Sam.

"I want to stay right here," she said.

"Where you going to hide anyhow," he said.

Sam put his book aside and turned out his light. He would pretend he was sleeping. Tillie snuggled in close, as close she could get without being inside him. He was a big man, and maybe if she got close enough, maybe they wouldn't see her. Outside, snow was falling through the radiant glows of the streetlight halos. Sam was warm, so warm, she felt his heat coming into her bones.

The snow outside reminded her of visiting Chester's grave in the early winter when the snow had just commenced, a soft snowfall like the one this night, white flakes falling on bare tree limbs. But then with Chester came thoughts of Lester Fiscus, which in turn brought the horrible Curly Smathers to mind. Of all the men in her life, they stood out. Her father too, of course. The wages of sin is death—one time he'd made her write that, *the wages of sin is death*, five hundred times on the blackboard of the Sunday school room at his church.

But Tillie isn't concerned. As she waits for them to come for her, she feels secure in the knowledge that everyone who calls on the name of the Lord will be saved, and so she knows she is saved. Sometimes she cannot even believe that it was her, that the person now inside her worn and wrinkled skin is the same woman who killed Curly Smathers. Surely it must have been someone else, another, earlier version of herself maybe, but someone else entirely from who she is today, another woman alone in the store those many years ago when Curly Smathers moseyed in to buy a Coca-Cola the day after the McCracken girls had vanished. Showed up calm as a can of peaches wearing a rag wrapped around his bald head. What was that woman to do? Her husband, Chester, in the hospital with his first heart attack. The shotgun loaded and handy behind the counter to protect herself while he was gone. Who could blame her? Who could blame her for eradicating that piece of evil from the face of God's earth when he sauntered up grinning to the counter, Coca-Cola in hand, a rag wrapped around his bald head, a rag of blue cloth with dark butterflies imprinted, a rag ripped from the sundress that Mary Lou McCracken had been wearing when she'd vanished the day before.

For that matter, who could blame her for cutting him up—there were axes, knives and saws galore in the store—into pieces small enough to fit through the hole in the outhouse seat, to dump him into the shit hole where he rightly belonged.

But the mess, the unholy mess. Tillie has finally stopped washing away the blood.

Quietly clutching Sam's warm, breathing body, she waits for them to come for her, her soul entirely cleansed. Outside, the clean, white snow falls on the home where all the old folks soldier on, on the whole town, on the countryside, on Chester's grave so far away.

Dennis McFadden grew up in Brookville, a small town in western Pennsylvania very much like the fictional Hartsgrove of *Jimtown Road*. He's a graduate of Allegheny College and is a project manager for the state of New York. He lives and writes in an old farmhouse called Mountjoy on Bliss Road, just up Peaceable Street from Harmony Corners in upstate New York. His stories have appeared in dozens of publications, including *The Missouri Review, New England Review, The Massachusetts Review, The Sewanee Review, Fiction, Crazyhorse, PRISM international, The South Carolina Review, Ellery Queen Mystery Magazine, Alfred Hitchcock Mystery Magazine* and *The Best American Mystery Stories*. His first collection, *Hart's Grove,* was published by Colgate University Press in 2010.

Cover artist Dawn D. Surratt studied art at the University of North Carolina at Greensboro as a recipient of the Spencer Love Scholarship in Fine Art. She has exhibited her work throughout the Southeast and currently works as a freelance designer and artist. Her work has been published internationally in magazines, on book covers, and in print media. She lives on the beautiful Kerr Lake in northern North Carolina with her husband, one demanding cat, and a crazy Pembroke Welsh Corgi.

CPSIA information can be obtained at www.ICGtesting.com
Printed in the USA
BVOW04s0522230916

462958BV00001B/2/P